Finding Moon Rabbit

A WAR.   A CAMP.   A GIRL.   A LETTER.

J.C. Kato and J.C.²

CHB MEDIA
PUBLISHER

Copyright © 2022 J.C. Kato & J.C.²

All rights reserved. No part of this publication may be reproduced, distributed, or transmitted in any form or by any means, including photocopying, recording, or other electronic or mechanical methods, without the prior written permission of the publisher, except in the case of brief quotations embodied in critical reviews and certain other noncommercial uses permitted by copyright law.

Finding Moon Rabbit is a work of historical fiction. References to historical events, real people, or real places are used fictitiously. Any resemblances in this work to real-life people or historical events should not be regarded as factual. The opinions expressed in this novel are those of the characters and should not be confused with those of the authors - nor anyone else.

Publisher's Cataloging-in-Publication data

Names: Kato, J.C., 1951- author. | C.², J., author.
Title: Finding moon rabbit : a war . a camp . a girl . a letter / by J.C. Kato & J.C.².
Description: Includes bibliographical references. | New Smyrna Beach, FL : CHB Media, 2022. | Summary: Homesick and missing her father, ten-year-old Koko adapts to life at a Japanese internment camp, learning how to obey while still doing the right thing. Identifiers: LCCN: 2021947697 | ISBN: 979-8-9852374-3-6 (hardcover) | 979-8-9852374-4-3 (paperback) Subjects: LCSH Heart Mountain Relocation Center (Wyo.)--Juvenile fiction. | Japanese Americans--Evacuation and relocation, 1942-1945--Juvenile fiction. | World War, 1939-1945--Concentration camps--Wyoming. | Family--Juvenile fiction. | BISAC JUVENILE FICTION / Historical / General| JUVENILE FICTION / Historical / Military & Wars | JUVENILE FICTION / Historical / United States / 20th Century | JUVENILE FICTION / People & Places / United States / Asian American Classification: LCC PZ7.1.K3723 Fin 2022| DDC [Fic]--dc23

Front cover art by Donna Kato.
Illustrations by Estelle Ishigo.
Book design by CHB Media (chbbooks.com).
Printed by IngramSpark, in the United States (and elsewhere).
First printing edition 2022.

CHB Media
New Smyrna Beach, Florida

Finding Moon Rabbit

For our Issei and Nisei of the KATO FAMILY

Unmitsu Kato, Hatsu Kanno Kato, Ichiro B. Kato, Mitsuko Maekawa Kato, Haru Kato Takeuchi, Masao Kato, Takeo Kato, Toshio Kato, Suyeko Kato Sugimoto, Roy Sugimoto, James Takeuchi

For our Issei and Nisei of the MAEKAWA FAMILY

Kaichi Maekawa, Rui Kimura Maekawa, Shinco Maekawa Collins, Mariko Maekawa Hashimoto, Magure Maekawa Nagai, George Maekawa

For our Sansei, Yonsei, and Gosei at home,
Denny, Donna, Kelly, and Ellie.

. . . with love and gratitude

One fine day, the moon god, disguised as a hungry beggar, decided to take a stroll on earth in search of kindness. A monkey climbed a tree to offer him fruit. Fox waded a stream to offer fish. Rabbit couldn't climb or swim, but his heart was earnest. He offered himself—and jumped into the beggar's fire.

— Japanese Legend of Tsuki no Usagi

NOTICE

Headquarters
Western Defense Command
and Fourth Army

Presidio of San Francisco, California
May 15, 1942

Civilian Exclusion Order No. 78

1. Pursuant to the provisions of Public Proclamations Nos. 1 and 2, this Headquarters, dated March 2, 1942, and March 16, 1942, respectively, it is hereby ordered that from and after 12 o'clock noon, P. W. T., of Thursday, May 21, 1942, all persons of Japanese ancestry, both alien and non-alien, be excluded from that portion of Military Area No. 1 described as follows:

   All of the County of Yolo, State of California, lying northerly and westerly of the northerly and westerly line of U. S. Highway No. 40.

2. A responsible member of each family, and each individual living alone, in the above described area will report between the hours of 8:00 A. M. and 5:00 P. M., Saturday, May 16, 1942, or during the same hours on Sunday, May 17, 1942, to the Civil Control Station located at:

   American Legion Hall,
   Bush Street,
   Woodland, California.

3. Any person subject to this order who fails to comply with any of its provisions or with the provisions of published instructions pertaining hereto or who is found in the above area after 12 o'clock noon, P. W. T., of Thursday, May 21, 1942, will be liable to the criminal penalties provided by Public Law No. 503, 77th Congress, approved March 21, 1942, entitled "An Act to Provide a Penalty for Violation of Restrictions or Orders with Respect to Persons Entering, Remaining in, Leaving or Committing Any Act in Military Areas or Zones," and alien Japanese will be subject to immediate apprehension and internment.

4. All persons within the bounds of an established Assembly Center pursuant to instructions from this Headquarters are excepted from the provisions of this order while those persons are in such Assembly Center.

J. L. DeWITT
Lieutenant General, U. S. Army
Commanding

THE FIRST DAY
August 12, 1942

Soldiers tell us the train's window shades must stay drawn, especially through towns.

They think if no one sees us, we don't exist.

Somewhere between California and Wyoming, I've decided to hate train rides. This isn't a quick trip to Sacramento with my sister to catch a movie, or when Mama needs special fabric and Pop film for his camera. It's more gut-twisting and bumpy like Dorothy's tornado ride to Oz—with the twisting and bumping part stuck inside my chest screaming, *Why did we have to leave our home?*

Homesickness lumps in my throat. My best friend, Charlene, will start sixth grade without me this year. How will I survive without her? Who'll bike with her to school every day? Who'll help me with arithmetic?

A bob of the train interrupts Mama's dozing. Worry has made lines around her eyes like tiny sparrow tracks left in snow. She peeks at Pop's pocket watch inside her purse. "We'll be there soon."

Part of me is glad our four-day ride is almost over. Another part would be happy to spend four more days cramped between Mama and Shirley eating baloney sandwiches if we could just return home to Clarksburg.

Home. Pop wouldn't be there, anyway.

Just days after war was declared against Japan, Shirley and I came home from school to find him gone, camera gear and all. "Your father's in Santa Fe on a photo assignment for Uncle Sam," Mama told us. "He'll be back as soon as he can."

Since December, we've been waiting for his letters to tell us when. *When?*

Mama said not to worry, but after New Years on February 19th everyone started to worry. President Roosevelt signed Executive Order 9066. It led to anyone, like me, with at least a sixteenth bit of Japanese blood to evacuate the Pacific West Coast.

It was for our own good.

The gentle swaying of the train rocks Shirley's head, loosening a silky black strand from her ponytail. I shift in my seat trying not to disturb her. I got used to being squished between them at Pomona Assembly Center. We slept in a horse stall together for almost three months waiting with thousands of other homeless people for our new houses to be built.

I liked my old house fine.

My homesickness returns and it's hard to swallow.

Mama's tulips aren't being watered. Shirley's record player isn't spinning Gene Autry songs, and spiders have probably moved in between the spokes of my bike.

"*Gaman*, Koko," Pop wrote in his last letter. "Patience."

If patience means a numb butt from riding so long on a train, then I have lots of *gaman*.

The clacking of train wheels slows. My pulse speeds up. I try to imagine our new house, and what it'll be like to live in a place called Heart Mountain. How bad could it be with the word "heart" in its name?

"Maybe we'll each get our own bedroom, Shirley."

"But I get first pick, Little Bug, since I'm a year older."

Her nickname for me falls warm on my shoulders. It's like a little piece of home she's brought with her to remind me that I'm me, Kokoro Marie Hayashi, and not a "Jap" like they say on the radio.

The train squeaks. Hisses. Jerks to a stop. A boy shouts, "We're here. We're here."

Dread weighs me down. Dorothy's house has landed.

I stretch, waking up my muscles. Mama thinks I've added at least another quarter inch since Pop last saw me, making me fifty-one and eleven sixteenth inches tall. I rub my neck. "I hope I remember how to sleep on a real pillow."

Shirley pulls our suitcases from the overhead storage space. "I hope the food's better here than at Pomona."

"A bath would be nice," Mama says. She adjusts the tag pinned to my coat. The government has given our family a number, as if we're prized cows at a fair. We're family number 20395. I'm 20395-D. D stands for being the youngest prized member of a family of three that should be four.

When the doors open, searing heat invades the stuffy train car. I blink from the bright sunlight while hundreds of us spill out like ants swarming from a nest. Soldiers wave us along with the butts of their rifles. Since before Pomona we've had to get used to guns, we just couldn't figure out at first who they were for.

They were for us.

"Follow the dirt road, people. Up the hill. Stop at the gate."

Mama holds tight to my hand. "We must do what they say."

The twister inside me screams, *Why?* But I know the answer:

Because I don't look like Charlene.

Wind pushes against my legs. Grit stings my face. Halfway up the hill, I look out over our Oz. There are no yellow-brick roads. No ponies. If I ever wondered what it was like to be stranded on the moon, it would look like Wyoming: Twisted brown mounds of earth as far as I can see. At the top of the hill is a sign.

HEART MOUNTAIN WAR RELOCATION CENTER

A lone mountain rises out of nowhere with a top shaped like a cowboy hat. In its shadow beyond a guard house and gate, are the houses we've been waiting for: rows and rows of black buildings the size of railroad cars lined up like dominos.

Mama stiffens beside me.

Tears fill my big sister's eyes, but she can't help it. There will be no soft pillows for our heads. No warm baths. No tasty food. I feel something draining from me and out my toes.

Maybe it's *gaman*.

I flick away tears so the soldiers can't see me cry. Someone needs to tell the President he's made a terrible mistake.

VOL. II No 1   2 Cents Within City 5 Cents Elsewhere

10,000 Heart Mountain Residents Greet 1943 With Mingled Feelings

Since the first evacuee set foot in Wyoming's newest and now third largest city back on the morning of August 12, a great change has come over the community of Heart Mountain.

What appeared to be chaos then has slowly but surely evolved into an orderly program of activity. Heart Mountain today is a smooth running, orderly and progressive city.

The evacuees have accomplished in the few short months since August more than they ever dreamed possible that fateful day last spring when evacuation was ordered.

The frigid Wyoming winter, accentuated by a sudden snow storm Monday night this week, re-emphasized to evacuees from balmy California that today little is as it has been ....

ICHI
Chapter One

When the howling wind outside quiets, the *tick-tick-ticking* of Pop's pocket watch fills the room. I lie still. Pretend he's here. When the wind picks up again, it drowns out the warmth of the sound, and I open my eyes to the bad dream none of us can wake from.

I slip from my covers and shiver to the window. Snow dusts the ground between our barracks. It's the end of March, almost a year since we left Clarksburg for Pomona, and three months since Pop's last letter.

> December, 1942
> Camp Santa Fe
> Santa Fe, New Mexico
>
> Heart Mountain Relocation Center
> Heart Mountain, Wyoming
>
> Dear Tomi, Shirley and Koko,
> I'm in good health. The Director says my work here should be finished by spring. Cross your fingers and toes.
>   Love Pop

He mentioned spring, but I don't think Wyoming will have one. It snows.

Rains.

Snows.

My breath fogs the windowpane, and I trace the outline of the mountain that watches over us. The morning moon hangs next to it in the sky. I circle my thumb and finger around my eye. Pop would like this shot. I *click* my tongue to snap it into memory for when he gets here.

Wake-up sirens slice through the camp's air, rattling my insides. I squint as the sound pierces my ear drums, as if cringing could make it stop. Sound marches us through our daily routines. All day. Every day.

Sirens and bugles for wake up.

Clanging bells for mess hall.

Whistles to start and finish work.

Bells to begin and end school.

Moans and yawns from the other five families that live here with us bounce across the rafters. Stove doors squeak open and closed. At the other end of the barracks in Unit B, the feet of Mrs. Yasaki's toddlers *thump-thump-thump* on the floor. Cardboard-thin walls separate the families, but there are no ceilings. When I look up, I see the same wood roof and beams that everyone sees at Barracks 20, Block 24.

We're in Unit C.

But I don't need a siren, bell or whistle to get me moving. Mama gave me the new job of hiking up to the Post Office before breakfast every morning. Any day now, a letter from Pop telling us he's on his way is bound to be there waiting for me to pick up.

Mama stirs, causing her to cough. "It feels too cold for you to go this morning, Koko."

I ignore the baby-bird noise her voice makes. It moved in when Pop's letters stopped. I hop from the window. "It's not too cold for me. Look, I'm already dressed."

She pushes aside the hanging Army blanket that separates her cot from the rest of the room and scans me head to toe. "You slept in the overalls I laid out for you last night?"

I smooth my wrinkled shirt sleeves. "I'm just doing what you told me by making better use of my time."

"That would be a miracle." Shirley grumbles from under her covers. "You daydream way too much."

Mama buttons my coat like I'm five years old, but I let her. Since Pop's been gone so long, she needs someone to fuss over and Shirley's too grouchy lately. I slip a finger inside my coat pocket to make sure the special letter I wrote last night is still there. It'll be a nice surprise for our family if it has half the luck I think it does to hurry Pop here. By Mother's Day would be great.

Mama finishes buttoning. "Now, where are your boots?"

I look at my socks. Wiggle my toes. Dorothy may have liked ruby slippers, but in this place, I'm happy to have a pair of boy's clodhoppers. Farm boots are important when you have to walk to the mess hall three times a day, shower, or you-know-what at the latrine.

Wyoming is hard on feet.

"Maybe I should wear Shirley's cowboy boots today."

"Over my dead body." My sister flips her covers off, ruffling the Gene Autry movie poster tacked on the wall above her bed. Red creases from sleep mark her face, making her look like one of Mama's cloth doll experiments. "I didn't lug them all the way from Clarksburg for you to ruin."

One hundred pounds of stuff per family was all we were allowed. My suitcase held my favorite sweater, overalls, saddle shoes, and all the *botan ame* rice candies left in the cupboard. I told Shirley not to forget her cowboy boots, and that's when she informed me that *her* boots were none of *my* business.

Without looking up, I know Mama's crinkling her eyebrows.

"You left your shoes outside again last night?"

I shrug. "They were too muddy."

Mama says all the mud in Wyoming is outside our door, and half of it sticks to my boots. She throws on her coat, ducks the crisscross lines of clothes hanging to dry, and whooshes out our unit door. Guilt clobbers me as she bangs the dried mud off my clodhoppers against the steps outside.

Shirley dresses under her bed covers. "If Mama gets sick again, it'll be your fault for making her go out in the cold to do something you should've done last night."

Her words sting with truth. It wasn't too long ago we both thought Mama would never get better, that her tuberculosis might be returning. "Sorry."

"Quit saying *sorry*, Little Frog, and pay better attention."

I ignore her new nickname for me. She doesn't mean it. When Mama was sick, Shirley carried the weight of the whole family on her shoulders. And when she found out that seventh-graders would attend high school at Heart Mountain she turned bossy.

Grouchy and bossy.

She hops from her bed and stubs her toes on my box of stuff. "Ouch!" She grabs her foot. "I thought you were going to take that junk to the lost and found."

"It's not junk."

She reaches past dolls with missing limbs, eyeglasses, toys, and grabs a handful of keys. "Koko, all this stuff, and these keys are useless to anyone. In case you haven't noticed, locks aren't allowed around here."

I push the box back against my bed where it should have been. "Just because things are lost or broken doesn't mean they're useless. What if someone's looking for these things."

She sighs, sits back on her bed still rubbing her toes. "You're sweet to want to maybe help someone, Koko, but there's nothing really fixable in your box. Sorry."

For a moment, it's my old sister from before camp talking to me, the one who used to play records with me, braid my hair, and dream under the moon of who we wanted to be when we grew up.

"But don't think you're fooling me, Little Frog," she adds, shifting moods. She grabs her brush and whips her long hair into a perfect pony-tail. "I know what's really going on here."

Grouchy. Bossy. Moody.

"You're finding this stuff while you're supposed to be in school."

My cheeks get hot. I hadn't thought she noticed. Some days when she walks one way to the high school and I walk the other to elementary, I just never make it. "It's not like real school," I say. "Real school is sitting at a real desk with real books and not freezing to death. Besides, Pop never made me go if I didn't feel good."

"Are you saying you're sick and that's why you're skipping school?"

"No. I'm saying that we're not supposed to be here in the first place, so I'm queasy all day without the throwing-up part." The outside barracks door opens. Mama's on her way back. "Are you going to tell on me?" I whisper.

She throws more coal in the stove. That's her job every morning, making a fire. "Maybe," she says, smiling. "Maybe not."

Mama's headscarf has slipped around her neck.

"Your boots are as clean as they're going to get." She holds them out to me.

"Thanks, Mama." I sit on my cot to lace up, and while no one's looking, I slip a hand under my mattress. When my fingers touch the soft ribbing of Pop's hiking sock, I breathe easier. Shirley hasn't found my other stash of lost things.

With boots laced, Mama ties my headscarf. "Come straight back now, and bring us good news."

Eleven times I've crossed the camp to the Administration Building and eleven times Mr. Oyama at the post office says, "No, Koko. No letter from your father."

Every time those words torpedo across the counter to me, I swear I'm never coming back. But little drops of *gaman* still stuck inside me won't let me give up.

I tap my coat pocket. Today will be different.

NI
Chapter Two

Mud sucks at my boots. *Ten, eleven, twelve* ... Mama says I can focus better if I count my steps. There are four-hundred-eighty of them to the Post Office, past twelve barracks, the latrine, showers, and a mess hall. There's a shortcut, but it's tricky knowing where the Military Police might be patrolling. The War Relocation Authority, WRA, makes the rules that the MPs make us follow, and they wouldn't approve of my shortcut.

Puddles stamped by thousands of feet shine like mirrors in the midway. One of them ripples, and I remember standing in my backyard with Pop showing me what to look for through the lens of a camera.

"Wait for a spark."

"That's silly, Pop. A tree swing can't spark."

"Sure it could." He checked through the lens. "Yep. For me it sparks the memory of the day I hung it for you and your sister." He winked and had me look again, but I'd already decided I wasn't cut out to be a photographer. He placed a reassuring hand on my shoulder.

A moment later, a tree swallow landed, wiggling the swing ever so lightly. It reminded me of the day Shirley thought I was ready for a push when I wasn't and landed on my face. We laughed so hard we peed our pants. "Got it, Pop," I said, and pushed the shutter button.

It was my last lesson before he left. I focus on the little mirrors in the mud, wait, focus—*click*.

At the administration building, a group of new arrivals relocating from other camps fill the hall. I don't know where they'll fit. Heart Mountain is already overcrowded. They look around at their surroundings and I know what they're thinking. *We are loyal Americans. What did we do wrong to end up here?* They huddle into little family packs marked by luggage and children tagged with numbers.

The numbers are so we don't forget who we are.

One of the WRA office workers is giving instructions to them. "We're a smooth running, orderly and progressive city here at Heart Mountain." His voice is as friendly as cold wind. "So long as you follow some basic rules."

More than anything, I want our family pack back together again, and my letter will help make that happen. It's already feeling lucky to me. I easily squeeze by everyone toward the post office and for once, the line to Mr. Oyama's counter is short. I step behind a man who's holding a little girl sound asleep. Slipping from her long braid that's draped over his shoulder is a blue ribbon tied in a perfect bow.

It's as blue and perfect as the ribbon I wore at Charlene's birthday party, Sunday, December 7, 1941. I look away hoping the memory will just fly by, but it lands like a bumble bee.

The birthday party had ended before cake. Ice cream melted untouched. We stood crying in our party hats listening to the radio speak of planes flying and bombs falling in that place with a funny name.

Pearl Harbor.

I'm snapped to attention with what the father says to Mr. Oyama. "We'll be sending a letter soon to my uncle. He'll be joining us from Santa Fe."

I inch closer, anxious to hear about the place where my father is helping Uncle Sam. This has been his longest photo assignment ever.

"Just make sure you post it by the end of the week," answers Mr. Oyama. "It'll be the last truck there for a while. WRA orders."

"Oh, is that because of the trouble they're having there and Tule Lake?"

I lean out of line to look at Mr. Oyama. "Trouble?"

The father turns and raises his eyebrows, surprised anyone's behind him.

"No. No trouble, Koko."

"But what kind of trouble isn't trouble?"

Mr. Oyama peers over his glasses. "The kind young girls don't need to worry about."

He sounds like my friend, Mr. Yamamoto, who's always telling me not to worry over things that can't be helped. He always says, "She gotta good eye." At least that's what the Japanese phrase sounds like to me in English. *Shikata ga nai.*

The father tips his hat to Mr. Oyama and rejoins the group. Finally. I'm next, and fidget with excitement. But Mr. Oyama is already wagging his head. The torpedo is on its way.

"Sorry, Koko. No letter from your father today."

I force a grin. *Gaman.* Pop had written to me. Patience. I close my eyes and picture all four of us sitting at the table near the potbellied stove. It gives me oomph enough to reach up and set my letter in front of Mr. Oyama. "Bet he'll write he's coming after he receives this."

He wags his head. "Clever, girl. With the war's paper shortage, who'd think to use the back of a jumbo-sized peach can label to write a letter?"

My spirits lift. The letter *is* lucky. "Mrs. Ishigo gave me the idea," I admit. "I saw her sketching on an applesauce label."

Mrs. Ishigo is one of the only *hakujin*, or Caucasians, locked up with us in camp. Women at the laundry say she was given a choice to live in or out of the camp, but she wouldn't leave her husband's side.

Love doesn't care whether you eat with chopsticks or a fork.

Mr. Oyama clears his throat. "You'll need an envelope and stamp, little girl," he says a little too loud.

My smile droops. I wanted to keep my letter a surprise and sometimes Mr. Oyama helps us out with stamps or envelopes. Mama had packed her piggy-bank stash, but without Pop and her being too sick to work, it's dwindled down low.

He leans over the counter. "Can't help you today, Koko," he whispers, nodding toward the crowd. "Someone's watching."

"We've got over ten thousand people here at Heart Mountain," the WRA man announces, "so we're tight for space. Couples and smaller families will have to double up, and you bachelors will have to bunk together. The social welfare department will notify you as more units become available." He begins to usher everyone out. "Block officers will show you to your assigned barracks."

Mumbles of disappointment and shuffling feet echo in the hall like it did the day my family arrived, except *that* day was hot. Today it's cold.

The sound is awful, either way.

"Something else, Koko." Mr. Oyama clears his throat. "Excuse me for reading your letter, but the Santa Fe camp would've probably struck black lines through your letter anyway. Especially the part about the guard."

I push my scarf down to cool my head. "But why would Pop let someone read my letter? He's working for Uncle Sam, you know."

Mr. Oyama clears his throat. "It's called censorship."

"Censorship?"

Thursday, March 25, 1943
Heart Mountain Relocation Center
Cody, Wyoming

Dear Pop,

This is to remind you it's almost April and spring is around the corner. Plus, Mama, Shirley, and I need you.

One night, our barracks door was buried by snow and we couldn't get out.

Another night when we returned from the latrine our barracks door was covered in ice so we couldn't get in.

Last week, we burned cardboard to keep warm. Shirley said we might as well burn the cake they make at the mess hall because it tastes just like cardboard. No sugar. (I think I saw a guard hide bags of it under his coat.)

I know you're helping Uncle Sam at Santa Fe, but please tell him we need you more at Heart Mountain. Surprising Mama on Mother's Day would be great.

And don't worry when the train stops at the bottom of the hill. It's a long walk up to the gate, but just remember, your family will be waiting for you on the other side!

Love,
Koko

P.S. I've been taking pictures in my head to catch you up on all that's happened since you've been gone. You'd better get here soon, though, or I'll forget.
XXOO

"It means they don't want to read about someone breaking rules no matter who they are." He slides my letter back across the counter. "Sorry."

My arms stiffen at my side. If I take my letter back, any luck I thought it had will disappear.

"Maybe you could write another letter about something good you're doing."

"Something good I'm doing?"

"Well, you go to school, don't you?"

I nod as if I do.

"You could write about how much you like your teacher."

"But I don't like my teacher."

He straightens. "Don't like your teacher?"

I hunch my shoulders. "One day Miss Percy told us she was pleased we spoke such good English, I answered, 'Of course we do, silly,' and she made me stand in the corner."

"Hm. I see. Well. You could write how you help Mr. Yamamoto, couldn't you?"

Mr. Oyama doesn't know that the best time for me to collect cans for Mr. Yamamoto is when I'm supposed to be in school.

"Or how you help your sister take care of your mother."

It's the last thing Mama would want me to say in a letter to Pop. She wouldn't want him worried—says she's getting better.

We both stare at the peach label that's stuck between coming and going.

"Maybe I can get your happiness back." He picks the letter up again. Flips it. Folds it. Flips. Folds. In less time than it takes for me to tie my boots, he's holding out a beautiful, peachy-colored paper heart. "You know Japanese *origami*, don't you?" he adds when I hesitate. "*Ori* means folding and *gami* means paper."

I know origami perfectly well. Though we may have been the only Japanese family in Clarksburg, I know that kimonos stay on without a single button, that *geta* sandals are meant to be worn in snow, and that "good morning" in Japanese sounds like "Ohio" in English. Since living in camp, I've learned that the number eight and a three-colored cat are lucky in Japan. I thought my letter would be lucky, too. Now it's just a pretty, peachy paper heart with words wrapped inside it that my father will never read.

I thank Mr. Oyama, slip the heart into my pocket, and head out to meet Mama and Shirley for mess hall. I'm warmed to my fingertips when I spot a familiar sliver of blue on a swirl of mud. The little girl's bow. It's a sign—a lucky sign.

I brush it off and slide it inside my pocket next to my paper heart. It'll be in good company with the other little things I've stashed away in Pop's hiking sock: a cigarette lighter, gō stones, cats-eye marbles, and a lady's hair comb with pearls.

I take a deep breath, encouraged. I'll write another letter—a better letter—full of good things the WRA censors will love to read.

A Page from the 1943 Girl Scout Leadership Handbook

SAN
Chapter Three

From the porch of the administration building, the shadow of the flagpole looming in the courtyard without a flag looks like a giant pencil without a letter to write. I scan for jobs in *The Heart Mountain Sentinel* newspaper that's posted outside.

> cooks—carpenters—
> beet farm workers—bookkeepers—
> electricians—block officers—

Tsk. Nothing for a girl who needs paper for a letter, a penny for an envelope, and a three-cent stamp. A gust of wind urges me to hurry. Mama and Shirley are waiting.

Thirty-three, thirty-four ... what to write in my new letter to Pop tip-toes into my steps. Mr. Kanabi walks ahead of me carrying a box of coal. His Navy surplus jacket hangs from his small frame. String is wrapped around his waist to keep out the cold. "Good morning, Mr. Kanabi."

"*Ohayo gozaimásu, Koko-san.*"

Speaking Japanese in camp is frowned on by the WRA, but Mr. Kanabi knows I'll never tell. He's *Issei*, or first generation of Japanese to live in America. I pick up coal he drops and hand it to him.

He nods a bow. "*Arigato.*"

I bow deeply in return to show respect. "You're welcome."

Idea for letter: Write how helpful and courteous I am.

Mrs. Gamachi pounds mud loose from her husband's overalls against the outside wall of her barracks.

"Hello, Mrs. Gamachi," I say in my sweetest voice and stretch-iest grin.

She frowns, disapproving of someone my age being so forward. She's *Nisei*, second generation born in America, like Mama and Pop. She speaks perfect English, just not to me.

Idea for letter: Write how friendly I can be.

"Hey, hey, wha'da'ya say, half-pint?"

I cringe and speed up. It's Marty Okamoto.

"I know you heard me, Koko."

"Unfortunately," I mumble. He thinks he's someone special just because his father's our security block officer. He must've cupped his hands to his mouth. "See you later, squirt."

He thinks he can tease me because I'm short for my age. I stomp a puddle without turning.

Idea: **Don't** write that Marty's a fathead.

Turning the corner, I'm happy to see my friend,

Mitzi Sakada, standing on her porch in white wooly socks two sizes too big for her. We met at school and have been pals ever since. She waves me over. "Let me guess. You're at step number one hundred, eighty-five, right?"

I nod even though I've forgotten all about counting. Wind fluffs her new movie star hairdo. We saw it in one of the magazines that the Red Cross gave us. It's cut above her shoulders and her mother let her get a permanent so it curls under. Bangs pinned away from her face show off her pretty eyes. Mama says I can get a perm, but I'm afraid Pop wouldn't recognize me.

"I only have a minute," I say.

"Me too. Mother wants me to help with *Baachan*."

A teensy pang of jealousy bubbles up at the mention of her grandmother. Pop's parents died while he was away at school in Japan. Mama's parents had to go back to Japan when she was eight, but she was too sick to go with them. Tuberculosis. Catherine Johnston, the lady they worked for, adopted Mama when my grandparents never returned. I pretend a sneeze to hide my watery eyes.

"You catching a cold?" Mitzi asks.

"It's just pollen."

Mitzi smiles. "Sorry, but uh, I'm pretty sure the sagebrush around here isn't pollinating."

Oops. I forgot. Her father used to own a flower shop—before the bus ride, train ride and long walk up the hill.

"Father says this soil could grow lots of food for the camp come spring."

I mush mud with my boot. When it dries, it'll look as dead as it did when we arrived in August. Her mother's call from inside makes us both look up. Mitzi's curls bounce as she turns to answer. "Coming, Mother."

My hair's too fly-away to bounce. Shirley was the one born with straight, shiny hair like Mama's. "I better go. Mama's waiting."

"Oh, but just one quick question first. Are you coming to the meeting later this week?"

"No. What meeting?"

She giggles. "Why do you say no to something before you know what it is?"

"I always say no first. That way if Mama says yes, it's a happy surprise."

"Well, I bet a million bucks your mother will say yes to this. It's about becoming a Girl Scout." She bounces on her toes like she's won a prize.

"Sorry, Mitz. You just lost a million bucks."

She scrunches her eyebrows. "What do you mean? Who doesn't like Girl Scouts?"

"Mama, that's who." I slide my hands up inside my sleeves to warm them. "The troop leader back home told Mama I wouldn't fit in the group even though the girls were in my class."

She looks up, like she's figuring fractions in her head. "Cuz' you're Japanese?"

I hitch a shoulder.

"That's lousy." Her tone tells me the same thing has happened to her.

"Mama told the troop leader that she should follow her own Girl Scout laws, like being clean in thought, word, and deed, and a friend to all."

"Your mother said that? To the leader's face?"

"Don't let Mama's looks fool you. She can melt shoes off a person with one glare."

"But I'm sure her mind's changed since, you know, since everyone here is Japanese. Well, except for the WRA people."

I shake my head no. "Every year I asked her, and every year she said the same thing."

"What?"

"Maybe next year."

Mitzi studies the ground. "But if my father gets to plant his garden, we could earn the Gardener badge. That's something she'd like, I bet." She takes a big breath. "And there's the badge everyone's talking about." She makes a circle with her thumbs and forefingers. "It's a patch with a crisscross of logs and fire embroidered on it, called the Campfire Badge. Just think, Koko, we could go camping!"

I'd like to be excited with her, but I'm not sure the person inside me who wanted to be a Girl Scout still cares. No matter how many badges I might have earned, President Roosevelt would have still signed his Executive Order 9066 that caused us to end up here.

"Sorry, but Mama would probably have a coughing fit just mentioning Girl Scouts again."

Her smile flattens.

Under my sleeve, I pinch my arm for making her unhappy. She's my friend. My best friend. My only friend in camp. "You know what, Mitz? You're going to make the best Girl Scout in all of Heart Mountain."

Her grin is worth the bruise I'll have on my arm tomorrow.

"You really think so?"

"Yep. You're honest and good, and never any trouble to your parents."

She beams. "Thanks, Koko." She tilts her head. "But promise you'll try to talk to your mother about the meeting?"

It's the last thing I want to do. "Sure."

She turns with a hop to go inside like it's a done deal. "Just think, we could be train greeters together."

"Train greeters?"

"Yeah. Some of the Girl Scouts will get special passes to leave camp and greet the people arriving on the train."

My heart beats so loud I bet she can hear it. "Really?" I picture the surprise on Pop's face when he steps off the train and sees a friendly face waiting for him on the platform.

I can't help but smile.

Idea for letter: Write how I'm going to be a Girl Scout train greeter with Mitzi!

YON
Chapter Four

The second siren stings the air. I have fifteen minutes to get back to 24-20. *Ninety, ninety-one, ninety-two* . . . I talked too long to Mr. Oyama and Mitzi, but it was worth it. My fingers touch the origami heart inside my pocket. "I'm going to be a train greeter," I say to it, and imagine my words tucked safe inside a new letter.

Mess hall bells ring all over camp.

I pick up my pace.

Maybe I should take my shortcut.

Better not.

But the MPs hardly patrol this end of the camp. It sits on a steep hill that slopes to a road. One way goes to Cody, the other to Powell City. Sunshine outlines the ridge of the Bighorn Mountains. Mr. Yamamoto said the Crow and Shoshone Indians rode horses along its spine long ago. Pop would like this shot, but I don't have time to stop.

I take my chances and hop around a corner, slip behind a junk pile, and then cross to the backside of a row of barracks. The rest of the shortcut is a piece of cake, except for the tricky part of not getting snagged by barbwire on my way to the other side.

Other side.

There was no *other side* when we arrived in August. Posts were dug and wire stretched in November. To keep us safe, they told us, from people in town who might mistake us for the enemy and shoot.

I shield my eyes from the brightening sun. Even with Shirley's warning inside my head, *don't do it, Little Frog*, I race to the fence, pull on the middle strand of wire, and slip through.

Barbs nip my finger, claw at my coat, but I'm small.

Fast.

And almost there.

"Hey you! Kid! Stop, or I'll shoot."

I freeze.

Boots crunch on the ground behind me.

Closer.

Fear spikes up my spine. I'm shaking—hardly able to keep my balance. A giant hand clamps my shoulder and I instantly know what a shirt feels like pinned to a clothesline. Fingers twirl me around.

"Where do you think you're going?"

I'm face to face with a wrinkly scowl and clenched teeth that I know all too well. Of all the guards in towers and MPs in jeeps patrolling the camp, the meanest one of all, stands in front of me. Maybe my shivering makes him release his hold, or maybe it's my very best performance yet of bawling.

"Stop crying, kid," he hisses.

I don't, hoping he'll feel sorry for me and let me go.

"You understand English?" he yells. He's so tall with crossed arms and steely look that he could be his very own guard tower. "Your blubbering's just going to make trouble for your family." He leans closer. "You want trouble for your family, kid?"

Piercing blue eyes pin me silent. Mid-sob, I stop.

His gaze narrows, shifting a toothpick from one side of his mouth to the other. "Didn't think so." He straightens. "I don't like troublemakers, see?"

I sniff and straighten, too. "I'm, I'm not a troublemaker."

He leans in again. "Yeah? Then what are you doing on the wrong side of the fence?"

It's hard to think with a toothpick in my face.

He waits.

I've forgotten the question.

"I asked, what are you doing outside the fence?"

My mind whizzes in circles for an answer. "Well, sir, um ..." I imagine Mama's worried face and Shirley's, *I told you so*. "You see, sir, I'm—um—" I have to think of something fast. "I'm a Girl Scout," I blurt out in a big fat lie. "A Heart Mountain Girl Scout."

His eyes narrow. "Girl Scout, huh?"

"Yes, sir. I'm working on a Pick-up-Trash Badge, and thought I saw something that needed picking up."

The lies dry out my mouth.

He turns an x-ray stare on me. "I can read a lie a mile away, you know." He studies me as if my fibs are piled too high to read through quickly. Then, he puts a hand on the back of my head. "Let's go."

We walk a long way to his Army jeep. After a few rough bounces and turns, it rumbles through the gate, down my street, and squeaks to a stop in front of 24-20. Mama's on the steps.

"Found your kid outside the fence, ma'am."

Mama's face is stern, like she's ready for a battle. She presses me close. Her insides tremble with mine.

"We've got orders to shoot anyone who tries to escape, you know."

She uses her worst, most shaming, how-could-you tone. "You people would shoot a little girl?" Even Mama's worst doesn't work on the meanest MP in camp.

"Now lady, does she look shot?"

She looks me over.

"She's fine," he says, annoyed. "Don't you know there's a war going on? WRA rules state that no one's allowed outside the fence."

"Yes, officer."

"It's corporal." He taps the stripes on his shirt sleeve. "Army corporal. Not officer."

I bury my face in Mama's coat and hook my arms around her. Hold tight.

"Yes, uh, corporal. We know the rules, and I assure you, my daughter's not trying to escape."

"Thing is, you people can't keep letting your kids run around unsupervised."

"Running an errand does not constitute running around. Koko is a good girl. A very honest and obedient girl."

Good, honest, obedient.

"Just telling you like it is, lady." He jumps back behind the wheel of the jeep. "If your daughter wanders off again, it'll be social welfare services knocking at your door."

Mama and I suck in breath at the same time. He revs up the jeep and drives away. Her hand tightens on my shoulder. The Social Welfare department is the last people we want knocking at our door.

久 久 久

Inside, Mama retreats behind the hanging blanket. I want to follow her, but it's her private space and I'm not invited. What would I say? Once a terrible thing has happened, how can you undo what you did?

"We'll need to catch up with your sister at the mess hall." I hear her changing clothes. "Did you hear me?"

My voice catches. "Yes, ma'am."

"What were you thinking? Who knows what that MP would have done? You might have gotten hurt. Shot!"

My stomach twists in a knot. I'm not the *good, hon-*

est, obedient daughter she'd like me to be. I've let her down.

"Sorry."

"Sorry isn't what I want to hear, Koko. Your sister's right. You daydream too much."

I hate it when she says my sister's right.

She steps from behind the blanket, tucking and smoothing clothes around her skinny frame. "Our days of daydreaming are over, Koko. They ended the day they forced us from our homes."

Looking out our window, the moon from this morning has gone to a place in the sky I can't see. We're like the moon. No one sees us, but we exist just the same.

Mama slips on her coat. "Do you *want* the social welfare lady at our door?"

No one likes to see the tall lady who carries trouble on a clipboard coming down the block. A knock on your door from her means your family is either too large or too small for your unit and will have to be moved. Our unit is short one member, and another move is sure to do Mama in. New determination makes my words louder than I want them to be. "No ma'am, I don't want the social welfare lady at our door."

"Then follow the rules."

The room fills with the ticking of Pop's watch. Mama sits at the table next to me and sighs. "Unjust rules are hard to bear Koko, but you can survive it all by holding your head up with dignity."

"I don't know how to do that, Mama."

"Sure you do." She smiles like she believes in me, even though I don't believe in myself. "You did it when we left Clarksburg, when we left Pomona, and when we stepped off the train at Heart Mountain.

"That was different. I didn't know what I was getting into."

"Dignity comes from following your own private rules, Koko." She takes my hands and soothes the top of them with hers. "Make them something you believe in, something good and right so that you'll never have to hang your head in shame for following them."

The scowl of the MP pops into my thoughts. "But it's that MP that should hang his head in shame." I huff the words out, but I know it was me who talked too long to my friends, and me who shouldn't have taken the shortcut.

Mama sighs and ties her headscarf. "Yes. He most certainly should."

I wrap my arms around her. "I promise, Mama. I'm never going to break another rule again." And I imagine my promise melting into her so she knows that this time, I really, really mean never.

GO
Chapter Five

The sun is getting higher and warmer as we make our way to meet Shirley. People cram the midway in one big noisy crowd. Three times a day, everyone on our block eats at the same time, same mess hall. WRA rules say absolutely no eating or cooking in the units. Mothers aren't even allowed a hot plate to warm milk for their babies.

Cooking is a fire hazard if you live in a matchbox.

A ticket gets you a meal, and Mama hands me mine. It's red, like the movie ticket I held for *The Wizard of Oz* when it opened in Sacramento.

It feels like a million years ago.

"There might be sewing for me to do with the Work Corps," Mama says as we walk. "I could earn twelve dollars a month, plus whatever I can make with extra mending." She squeezes my hand. "I promise to do better too, Koko."

Our promises to each other feel as real as rainbows. I return her squeeze. "I never want to let you down again." I look for any shadow of left-over anger in her face. None is there, but wheezing has tip-toed into her breathing.

Boys race by us, making us lean out of their way. They've already eaten at their block's mess hall and are headed toward ours for an illegal second helping. Where are the MPs when you really need them?

People glare as we skip in line with Shirley. She's laughing with an older girl I've never met, but her laughing stops when she sees us.

"What's wrong? What's Koko done now?"

I wonder if riding in an MP's jeep is scribbled on my face.

"Nothing," Mama says, smiling. "Koko was a little late, but here we are."

Mama's found a way to tell the truth without the bad parts. "Yep. Here we are."

Shirley looks sideways at me. "No fooling?"

I put a hand on my hip. "Are you saying you don't believe our mother?"

"*Ohayo gozaimásu*," says the girl Shirley was talking to.

Shirley's frown reverses. "Mama, this is my new friend, Yuki Fujikawa. She's the one I told you is *Kibei*, like Pop. She was born in L.A. but went to school in Japan."

I can believe Yuki's from Los Angeles. She's almost a head taller than my sister, and her black hair is shaped in a Bette Davis style showing off her large eyes that kiss in the corners.

"It's nice to meet you, Yuki," Mama says. "Though, I'm sorry it's under these circumstances."

"Oh, but I'm not sorry, Mrs. Hayashi. I never liked school in Japan." Yuki turns her body so her parents who are in line ahead can't hear. She lowers her voice. "My parents are very old fashioned about *e-ver-y-thing*. Luckily we were visiting my uncle when the Japanese dropped the bombs. . . ." She looks down.

We all stiffen at her big social boo-boo.

Here at Heart Mountain, we complain about the fickle weather, gripe about the mutton stew, and ask who's getting married, but no one—I mean no one—mentions the worst day of everyone's life.

December 7th.

Yuki giggles. "I mean, certainly I'm not glad for the bombing, I just meant I'm glad I don't have to go back to Japan." A look of desperation waves over her pretty face and she looks to me to be her life raft. "Oh Shirrrl, your little sister's sooo cute."

I bite my tongue. She's actually shortened my sister's name to sound like hamster noise, and it's already been shortened enough from Kazuko. Kazuko Shirley Hayashi.

"This is Koko," Shirley says.

I want to swat Yuki's hand away when she pats my head like I'm a little kid, but I know what it's like to make boo-boos. "I look little," I say, feeling sorry for her, "but I'm old." It's the answer I give to everyone until I have the growth spurt Mama keeps promising me.

"Wish they'd open the doors," says Shirley. "I'm starved."

My stomach growls in agreement, but I'm still too upset to eat. A jeep ride before breakfast, and the racket of over two hundred people sitting in one place, sours the thought of food.

Finally, the doors open. A waft of baked bread and hot grease passes over us. Inside, pots and plates and silverware clank. The room pops with the lively conversations of three generations of Japanese in America—*Issei* and *Nisei* and third generation, us—*Sansei*—speaking in Japanese, English, or half of both at the same time. It's toasted bread and powdered eggs today. We carry our trays to picnic tables butted end to end. There's no jam or jelly on the table. No Log Cabin syrup. No Cheerios. Mama and I sit next to Shirley, who's busy talking to Yuki like we don't exist.

WRA rules ruined family mealtime.

At first, fathers insisted their family sit together. But the rush to get in, grab a plate, eat fast, and scoot out to make room for others, makes it hard for families to sit together. Mama tried her best to keep the tradition going. Even when she wasn't well enough to make it to mess hall, Shirley and I promised her we'd sit together.

Shirley jabbers away with Yuki as Mama quietly eats her bread. I push my disgusting powdered eggs around on my plate and wonder how a senior and seventh-grader find so much to talk about. If Mitzi and I ate at the same mess hall, we'd be jabbering too. Maybe.

Mitzi would never let her parents eat alone.

I look at Mama. Me neither.

久 久 久

"This is where we leave you, Little Frog."

"I know."

"Straight to the elementary school barracks, right?"

"I know."

"Wow, Shirrl," says Yuki. "I wish my older sister worried over me like that." She tilts her head and pats my head again. "It's only a few blocks, Koko. You'll be okay."

I bite my tongue. Just because I'm small doesn't mean I can't take care of myself.

"And don't—

"I know—*Shirrl*. Don't daydream."

Those days are over. They ended the day the bombs fell, but that was then and this is now.

ROKU
Chapter Six

Forty, forty-one, forty-two ... It's been so long since walking to school, I don't remember how many steps it is to class.

Lots of kids missed school when the camp first opened. Every blizzard—stay home. Coal shortages—stay home. Flu outbreak—stay home. And when Mama got sick—I stayed home. I was out of school more times than not, and after a few more visits with Miss Percy's classroom corner, I decided I wouldn't be missed.

Fifty, fifty-one, fifty-two ... This street is where I usually double back to the mess hall dumpsters. After breakfast and before lunch is the best time to find cans for Mr. Yamamoto. I don't know why he needs them, but he's glad when I show up with a potato sack full.

The first school bell rings. I walk faster. *Fifty-five, fifty-six, fifty-seven* ...

I pass the canteen. It sells real food, like ice cream and fresh fruit—if you can afford it. The old *Issei* men sit on the porch around makeshift tables playing their daily game of *gō*. No time to stop and watch them rub their stubbly chins and tap stones on the board before each move.

Sixty-three, sixty-four, sixty-five ...

People stand in a long line holding blue tickets at the shoe repair shop. *The Heart Mountain Sentinel* reported that a thousand shoes had been repaired since Christmas.

I'm almost to my school building when the pop of guns suddenly fire. I duck.

"Last day of MP target practice for the month," a man in the shoe line says.

A woman behind him answers. "*Tsk*. Practice for what?"

Remembering the weight of the MP's hand on my head reminds me *for what*—to shoot anyone on the wrong side of the fence.

Today, it could have been me.

Mitzi waves from a group of students and waits up for me. "Is your mother feeling better?"

I swallow hard. I've told her I miss school to take care of Mama, which was true for only some of the time.

Note to self: No more fibbing, especially to a friend.

"Your cheeks are as red as roses," she adds. "Aren't you hot?"

"I didn't have time to change. Mama walked with me to the mess hall, and she walks slow."

"Bet the warmer temperature today has something to do with her feeling better. Father says it's going to get even warmer by the end of the week, and you know what that means don't you?"

She doesn't wait for my answer.

"Gar-den-ing time," she sing-songs. "My father's idea for a garden will lift everyone's spirits."

Sometimes I'm jealous when Mitzi talks about her father. My hand feels for the origami heart still in my pocket. I like thinking the four corners of the folded paper are like the four members of my family tucked safely together.

Inside the classroom, no one's fighting for a seat closest to the stove. The camp's carpenters have built more desks since the last time I was here. But the best ones at the back of the room are still hogged by Millie, Fusa and Ruth from Block 30. They're another reason I didn't mind missing school. They act bossy with me because they're taller, and I already have enough bosses in my life.

When a special visitor to the class arrives, I offer my chair, and Mitzi sits next to me on the floor.

Miss Percy taps a ruler. "Attention, children. I'd like you to welcome Miss Johansson, Heart Mountain's librarian."

I've been missing out. I didn't know a library had even opened. Charlene and I used to stop at the library every day on our way home from school, even if we didn't have homework. Miss Johansson doesn't even look like a librarian. She doesn't wear horn-rimmed glasses, is pretty, slender, and wears a stylish twist. Unlike Miss Percy who doesn't care how unruly her straw curls get.

Miss Johansson stands with hands poised in front of her as if she's about to sing a solo. "Thank you, and good morning, children." She clears her throat. "As you know, when you all first arrived, the only books in camp were the ones you carried here from your homes."

I had put my copy of *Carmen of the Golden Coast* by Madeline Brandeis in my suitcase, then took it out—put it in—out. I couldn't take just *one* book off my shelf and leave *Thimble Summer* and the other *Children of America* books. It would've been like breaking up a family.

"Thanks to the donation of people and schools from all over the country, I'm proud to say that Heart Mountain Library now has over four thousand books on its shelves."

I wonder if my old library or school sent books. Homesickness wells up in me. Sadness drapes over my heart like a heavy blanket.

Clarksburg was so small, no one really believed our family would have to evacuate. *What harm could we be?* But I wasn't the only kid shocked when the two FBI men wearing fedora hats came for me during arithmetic. Kids I'd known all my life suddenly stared at me like I was a stranger. Charlene jumped to place herself between them and me, as if her blond pigtails and white skin could protect me somehow.

I almost loved her more than my own sister in that moment, and that's saying a lot.

While Miss Johansson speaks to the class, I try to listen, but other thoughts float in, like the list of my own private rules I want to follow.

1. Keep promises.

2. Try your best not to fib, especially to friends.

3. Follow rules.

4. Pay attention. (Daydream at the library.)

5. Be on time.

6. AVOID MPs AND SOCIAL WELFARE LADY.

"And, children," Miss Johansson continues, "something fortuitous has happened." She pauses to take a big breath. "This morning I was informed that a valuable set of Encyclopedias will be donated to the library!"

The kids *oooahh*. Mitzi whispers, "Aren't those the same encyclopedias you found thrown away, Koko?"

I'd stood on the box containing them to reach the peach label from the dumpster. It bothered me that someone would throw books away.

"I told Mr. Oyama," I whisper back to Mitzi. "He must've told one of the *hakujin* in the office and they must've told you-know-who, Mr. Boss of all *hakujin* Bosses of Heart Mountain."

"You mean, Mr. Henderson?"

"Yeah, the big guy whose necktie always looks too tight."

"Well, he should have at least told the librarian that you were the one who found them in the first place."

I nudge Mitzi, playfully, wondering if she knows it's not her movie star hairstyle that makes her a star in my book. She nudges me back.

When Miss Johansson finishes her talk, she invites everyone to visit the library, and then Miss Percy makes an announcement.

"In light of the new encyclopedias, I'm giving you a writing assignment."

The class groans. She must have not heard there's a paper shortage.

"Now don't fret, children. It's not due until Tuesday, May 11th, which is six weeks away. That's plenty of time for you to finish. It's the same day the camp will celebrate getting a new flag."

I remember the flagpole's lonely shadow at the administration building.

Marty Okamoto's little brother, Kenny, sits with the third-graders on the floor, and wiggles his hand in the air. "Guess what, Miss Percy, guess what? My brother's playing bugle for the flag ceremony. He's a Boy Scout."

"See, Koko?" Mitzi whispers. "Scouts do important things."

"Yeah, that's why I'm going to be a train greeter."

"Miss Hayashi?"

Miss Percy stands over me with an arched eyebrow. "We're glad your mother must be feeling better, and that you could join us today, but we still have the rule of not speaking out of turn in class. Is there something you'd like to share with all of us?"

The girls in the back of the room snicker like they usually do, and I usually tell them to keep their snickers to themselves, but things have changed. I've made a promise to Mama.

I clasp my hands in front of me. "No, ma'am."

Miss Percy returns to her desk and reaches into her bag. I forget any scolding she's ever given me when I see what she's holding.

Writing paper.

Beautiful, white writing paper. It's funny how you don't realize how precious something is until you don't have it anymore.

She hands the stack to Mitzi. "Miss Sakada will be passing out three sheets of paper to each of you. Two sheets are for practice and one is for your assignment to turn in. You all know there's a paper shortage, so make each sheet count."

I consider it *fortuitous*, like the librarian said. It's a sign—another lucky sign—that I'll be able to send off a new letter to Pop by the deadline.

I wave my hand. "What do you want us to write, Miss Percy?"

"Write about an American you admire, and why you admire them."

I know exactly the American to write about—Pop. The words tumble easily into my head. I'll write about how he's volunteered to help Uncle Sam at Santa Fe, or how he loves taking pictures. I could write about the time he saved a baby eagle, or helped raise money for our neighbors when the Sacramento River flooded and washed their house away.

"The only rule," Miss Percy adds, "is that the American you write about not be a family member."

Her rule and my Rule 3: Follow rules, crash inside my head.

"Did you talk with your mother yet about the meeting?" whispers Mitzi.

Another crash. Rule 1: Keep Promises. The only mention of Girl Scouts this morning was when I lied to the MP about being one. "No. I forgot." My stomach hurts. I'm not ready to ask Mama about Girl Scouts, but how can I keep my promise to Mitzi if I don't?

She holds up her pinkies. "Promise you'll talk to her soon?"

She's going to make me do our sacred, do-or-die Double-Shake-Pinkie Promise. We cross our arms, grab each other's pinkies, and shake twice.

Now I have to keep my promise, or die.

HEART MOUNTAIN SENTINEL

VOL. I No. 7   2 Cents Within City 5 Cents Elsewhere

Girl Scouts Take Orders for Cookies

"Lookee, Lookee, Lookee, here comes Cookie!" The Girl Scouts have started their cookie drive!

From early this morning the Brownies, intermediate and senior scouts have begun canvassing each home with 1,000 boxes of cookies as their ultimate goal.

Each box contains 44 cookies in an assortment of chocolate and vanilla flavors. The price per box is 25 cents.

SHICHI
Chapter Seven

It's been a week since I've visited Mr. Yamamoto. Even before my personal list of rules, I had already promised Mr. Yamamoto I'd bring him as many cans as I can find. This afternoon, they clunk inside my potato sack in rhythm to my steps. He told me cans are vital to our survival, and he knows lots about surviving.

When snow fell for a week and blocked our door, he was the one who dug us out. When winter iced our door shut, he chiseled it open. And when Mama got sick, he delivered coal to our doorstep every day. I don't know when he adopted us or we adopted him, but since the first day at Heart Mountain, he's been like an *ojīsan,* or grandfather, to me. One day when he caught me crying for Pop, he never told me things would be all right. He told me how, not so far away in Yellowstone Park, big herds of buffalo roam free and raise their young. That hot, bubbling pools of acid water where you'd think nothing could survive, teem with life. And that grizzly bears not only survived the last ice age, but its population grew.

So when he says cans are vital to our survival, I believe him.

I find him sitting on his roof.

"What are you looking for up there?"

"Not looking. Listening."

I tilt my ear up. "To what?"

"The Shoshone river."

I remember seeing the river when I peeked under the window blind of the train.

"Snow from the mountain is melting fast into the river," he says. "It roars like a lion, but as it churns the soil, it looks like chocolate milk."

Gushing chocolate milk makes me wish I had some. The mess hall serves powdered milk and sometimes watered-down evaporated milk, but it's never chocolate. Mr. Yamamoto recites a poem like he's on a mountaintop instead of a roof. I call it his sky talk.

He says, "*haru no umi*"

He's waiting for me to repeat each line so I can try out new Japanese words. I'm not very good.

I answer, "har-oo noh oo-me"

"*hinemosu notari*"

"heen-eh-moh-soo noh-tar-ee"

notari Kana"

"noh-tar-ee kah-nah"

"Buson wrote that long ago," he says. "It's *haiku*."

It sounds like a sneeze.

"The sea at springtime.

All day it rises and falls,

Yes, rises and falls."

Pop loved taking shots of the sea. I think he'd understand Mr. Buson's *haiku*. He'd probably like sitting on Mr. Yamamoto's roof, too.

"Where's Mitzi?"

"She's helping her mother with her *baachan*."

"Ah. Mitzi's a good girl."

I shield my face from the sun. "Please climb down, Mr. Yamamoto. I have cans for you."

"No need to call me Mr."

"Mama says I should be respectful to old people."

"Ha. Yes. I'm verree old."

My neck aches from looking up. "You don't like your name, Mr. Yamamoto?"

"At Berkeley, *hakujin* bosses say, 'Yamamoto, roll up maps. Yamamoto, carry this, carry that.' For thirty years I worked in America, learned English, learned its geology, but it never let me be a 'Mister'. Never a citizen."

I give my neck a rest and look out at Heart Mountain. The Native people named it for looking like the heart of a buffalo. Mr. Yamamoto calls it a misfit mountain because it blew off from a mountain in Montana and fell *kerplunk*, right here. We landed here *kerplunk*, too.

"Call me Yama-san," he says, startling me from behind. His balding head is sunburned, and he grins so big his eyes almost disappear. "Not too old for climbing down roofs, yes?"

I offer him my sack of cans. "I haven't had as much time to find more."

He's smiling just the same. "Ahh, *arigato*. Want tea?"

Mr. Yamamoto lives in a space in a storage building not far from his block's mess hall. He's supposed to share a unit with bachelors, but his secret's safe with me. He waters a little plant sitting in the windowsill and offers me a seat inside, an empty nail crate. On a shelf, next to my head, is a buffalo skull. Draped over it, is a long, long link of rattlesnake skin.

"I was worried the MPs would shoot you, Yama-san," I say, practicing his new name.

"*Ashee*. Why shoot an old man?" He pours me tea in a tin cup.

"I know it can happen, because one almost shot me last week."

Mid-pour he knits bushy eyebrows together. "Why shoot a little girl?"

I hitch a shoulder. "Don't know." The fib tastes bitter on my tongue, and I've broken Rule 2: Try your best not to fib, especially to a friend. "I mean, yes, Yama-san. I do know why. I was taking a shortcut that happened to be a little on the other side of the fence."

He shakes his head. "That explains your long *kabuki* face."

"*Kabuki?*"

"You know, Japanese theater? Feelings painted on a face like a mask?"

"No. This is my same old Koko face, just worried more."

He sits on his cot and slurps his tea.

I slurp.

He slurps.

Slurping is a Japanese way of complimenting the chef.

"Mama says I need to follow rules better."

He studies the steam from his tea. "*Hai*. Guards obey rules. Shoot good."

"*Hai*," I answer, liking how the Japanese word sounds like "Hi!" but means yes in Japanese. Another sip of tea. "I lied to an MP," I say, spilling out words I hadn't planned on sharing. "I told him I was a Girl Scout."

He raises a brow. "What's a Girl Scout?"

"Someone who, you know, follows honor, duty—doing good stuff."

"*Hai*." He gulps the rest of his tea and smacks an *aaahhh*, like it's the best tea he's ever had. "Honor, duty. Sounds like old *samurai* talk."

I slurp and *aaahhh*. "A friend of Shirley's told her that in old Japan, if a new shogun took over a village, the people would have to follow their new rules or get their heads chopped off. Is that right, Yama-san?"

"*Hai*. WRA is our new shogun. Except we lose

freedom and dignity. Not head. Hmph. Might be the same."

I fidget on the crate. "Do you think if I'm a Girl Scout, I'll never fib without thinking again?"

"Having good reflexes is no crime, Koko."

"You mean fibbing's a reflex?"

"No. Reflex from fear, sometimes pops out like fibs."

"Mitzi never pops out fibs."

"Ah. That Mitzi's a good girl."

The tea in my cup's gone cold. If only I was as good as Mitzi. "She and I are going to be train greeters together."

He tilts his head. "Huh?"

"A train greeter. You know, someone who greets the train at the bottom of the hill?"

"This is a veerry good plan." We tap cups. "You'll be the best train greeter in all of Heart Mountain."

Warmth rises from my heart. Visiting Yama-san began because I didn't want him to be alone, but I'm the one who's thankful.

A scratching noise comes from under his cot. "Do you have rats, Yama-san? I've seen lots of rats running around camp lately. They bite, you know."

"Nope. No rats here."

More scratching. "You don't hear that?"

"It's a secret weapon."

"Secret weapon?"

"*Hai.* To lift your long face." He points to a box under his cot.

It whines.

I stand.

Yama-san slides the box out. A pair of innocent blue eyes and black snout pokes out over the edge of the box. A puppy!

"Meet Berkeley."

I squeal. "Where'd you find him?"

"Delivery driver found him near the road. No mama."

Berkeley nuzzles my ear, and his breath smells as free as a warm Wyoming night. It lifts me up and away, over the roofs of barracks, past the MP towers, and all the way home to Clarksburg.

"My secret weapon works good, yes?"

My thoughts drift for a while, and then return. "But what if Berkeley's spotted by the WRA? He'll be taken away. Or shot!" I hold him tighter. "The guards are always target practicing."

He shakes his head. "No one comes up this far, except you."

Berkeley's scratchy pink tongue tickles my neck. "But having a dog is against rules."

"Don't worry, Koko-san. I'm breaking rules, not you."

Berkeley suckles my fingertips. "He's just a little lost baby," I say, looking forward to seeing him again.

"A baby is like a happy promise that a better future is coming, yes?"

Love can arrive in an instant, precious and innocent. Berkeley is definitely a promise I want to keep. I pet his tiny snout. "Don't worry, little guy. You have a family now."

HACHI
Chapter Eight

Wyoming wouldn't be Wyoming without wind, and when it doesn't blow, it feels like something's wrong. Today when we step out of the classroom, it whips hard and frosty. Scarves flap and skirts balloon like windsocks. That's why I like overalls, to keep my legs from becoming popsicle sticks. I hate to be cold, and I've worn my coat just in case.

Before the Girl Scout meeting this afternoon, Mitzi insists on squeezing in a library visit to get going on our American assignment. "Never put off till tomorrow what you can do today."

"But it's not due for weeks, and my goose bumps have goose bumps. Aren't you cold?"

"Freezing. But the sooner we start, the sooner we can focus on my father's garden."

When the library door closes behind me, a rush of warm air melts my resistance. Libraries must smell the same everywhere, inky and good, with a special kind of quiet from people reading. If there's a place in the whole camp that comes close to reminding me of home, it's here.

Miss Johansson greets us. "You two are just in time. A group of teachers from the City of Powell sent us several boxes of books today that you might enjoy reading."

Books fill the shelves with stories that won't remind us of the awful place we're stuck in. I browse the aisles and find a copy of *Carmen of the Golden Coast*. I tip it out for a look, but let it fall back into its space. Just me touching it feels disloyal to my own copy at home stuffed in a box with my other books. I find *Black Beauty* by Anna Sewell, Shirley's favorite. Maybe reading it again will make her less grouchy.

I put that back, too. I slip my hand in my coat pocket and realize the origami heart, my letter to Pop, is still there. I pull it out to look at it. It would make a good bookmark. "Do you have any *haiku* books, Miss Johansson?"

She raises her eyebrows. "I don't know. Let's look." After a quick search, she hands me a book of poems by Emily Dickinson. "They're not haiku, but they're short like haiku."

Mitzi looks over my shoulder as we page through.

"Dickinson wrote many of her poems while looking out her window," Miss Johansson adds. I wonder if looking out the window at Barracks 20, Block 24 will turn me into a poet.

"Hey, Mitz. Here's a poem about a garden." We read it together.

> *New feet within my garden go,*
> *New fingers stir the sod;*
> *A troubadour upon the elm*
> *Betrays the solitude.*
>
> *New children play upon the green,*
> *New weary sleep below;*
> *And still the pensive spring returns,*
> *And still the punctual snow!*

"See?" she says. "We're the new feet and fingers for the garden here at Heart Mountain."

Writing about Emily Dickinson for my American assignment would be good, but I can't get out of my head what I want to write about Pop. I tug on Mitzi's sweater sleeve. "Let's hurry to the Girl Scout meeting. I can't wait to start greeting those trains."

Library at Heart Mountain, Estelle Ishigo

"Hello, girls," says the woman at the door. "I'm Mrs. Somekawa."

I'm stumped for words.

Many people in camp are from Los Angeles, but this lady must be from Hollywood. Pink lipstick matches her blouse, a pretty scarf is tied around her neck, and she wears slacks. I tuck a fly-away hair under my scarf.

We place our shoes by the door, next to others. All the B units are the same, but this one has matching curtains and bedspreads with furniture probably ordered straight out of the Montgomery Ward Catalog.

"My sister is the one passing out cookies," says Mrs. Somekawa. "Miss Makabe will be our assistant scout leader."

I recognize Miss Makabe by her glasses. She works for the Boss of All Bosses, Mr. Henderson. She translates for the *Issei* who don't speak English. "Hi girls," she says. She offers cookies to three girls already here that I'd rather not see: the desk-hoggers from school, Millie, Fusa and Ruth. "As Girl Scouts, you'll be selling cookies, you know."

I haven't had a chocolate cookie in so long, I stare.

Mitzi nudges me. "Didn't I tell you joining Girl Scouts would be great?"

I feel my mouth watering as I lick its icing.

Mrs. Somekawa passes out slips. "These are consent forms for your mothers to sign in order for you to attend the meetings."

Cookie catches in my throat. Mama doesn't even know I'm here. I'd hoped after I got a few meetings under my belt that she would notice how much I've changed for the better. Then I could tell her how it was Girl Scouts that did the trick.

The taller girl in the middle of the threesome dabs cookie from her lips. "Excuse me, ma'am," she says. "My name's Ruth Niwa, and I thought you had to be ten years old to join Girl Scouts." As the last word leaves her mouth, she swivels her head to look at me, using a smile as fake as she is. She knows very well how old I am.

"I'm old enough," I say, to set the record straight.

"Good. That's settled," says Mrs. Somekawa, and opens a Girl Scout manual. "Now, you all should know that everyone must learn the Girl Scout Promise and Laws, which is part of the Code of Citizenship."

Ruth raises her hand. "Oh, I already know the Girl Scout Laws." She stands and reels them off from the first law about a Girl Scout being trusted all the way to Mama's favorite: to be clean in thought, word and deed.

The girl sitting next to Ruth raises her hand. "My name's Fusa Mineta, and I've memorized the Girl Scout Promise by heart." She stands and recites it excitedly.

Mitzi introduces herself, and then it's my turn. "My name's Kokoro Catherine Hayashi." I give a little bow, but my scarf slips. Static electricity snaps, and I know my hair must be sticking out like cobwebs.

The desk-hoggers snicker.

I sit, wishing I'd never given Mitzi our sacred Double-Shake-Pinkie Promise.

The other girl of the threesome raises her hand. "My name's Millie Sugimoto and my mother said we might go hiking outside the fence."

I sit at attention. "What? And get shot?"

"*Tsk*. How ridiculous, Koko," says Ruth. "No one would shoot a Girl Scout."

Defending myself would only lead to me explaining how I know, better than anyone in the room, what happens on the *other side* of the fence.

Miss Makabe pulls out a notebook. "How about we talk about badges." She pushes up her glasses. "I've made a schedule of activities happening in camp that might be good opportunities for you to earn badges. For instance, Mr. Henderson has announced a camp clean-up week, which could be a Community Safety Badge. How does that sound?"

Someone must've nodded. She makes a big check in her notebook. "And, there's an art contest planned for May. Would you like to work toward an Arts and Crafts Badge?"

"Oh, I've got a million ideas for something to paint," says Ruth.

Check.

I'm not very crafty. But I wonder if Mama would show me how to stitch a quilt scene the size of a pillow with her cloth scraps. I imagine our table by the stove with a window view of Heart Mountain. I'd pick orange and brown cotton to be the ground outside, tan for our floor, a tiny flower print for the curtains, maybe some blue silk from someone's old kimono for the sky, and a brown piece of corduroy cut in the shape of a cowboy hat for Heart Mountain.

"A songfest is scheduled for Mother's Day. How about a Music Appreciation badge?"

Check.

Mitzi raises her hand. "I've got a keen idea for a badge, Miss Makabe, don't I, Koko?"

Everyone looks at me, waiting. "Um, what was it, again, Mitzi?"

She giggles and nudges me with her elbow. "You know, silly. My father's garden?"

Mrs. Somekawa claps. "Oh perfect. Write the Gardener Badge on your list, sis."

Check.

Ruth raises her hand. "My mother's ordering a flag for our Investiture Ceremony. It's one hundred percent silk."

"Investiture?" I ask. "What's that?"

Ruth rolls her eyes. "You don't know what an investiture is?"

The silence is as prickly as standing in Miss Percy's corner.

Miss Makabe saves me. "It's a ceremony commemorating the completion of your training as a Girl Scout. Kind of like the ceremony given to our soldiers who finish their Army boot camp training."

I hesitate. The *Nisei* boys joining the Army is a hot topic at the laundry room. The mothers argue as they scrub. I call them the *yes-yes* mothers and *no-no* mothers. The *yes-yes* mothers want their sons to be good citizens and join the Army even though their families are all locked up here. The *no-no* mothers want their sons to be good citizens and *not* join the Army because their families are all locked up here, too. "Okay, just so long as I'm not joining the Army."

Ruth laugh-snorts. "What a silly thing to say." Her friends laugh, even Mitzi.

"There's something else my sister and I are planning," says Mrs. Somekawa. "We'll need final approval from Mr. Henderson, of course, but the troop leaders in camp have designed a merit-based program for Girl Scouts to be train greeters."

Check! My hand shoots up like a firecracker. "Oh please. I want to be a train greeter more than anything!"

"Now that's the kind of enthusiasm I like to see," says Mrs. Somekawa.

When Mama finds out that by joining Girl Scouts, I might be able to greet Pop at the train, she's bound to say yes.

KU
Chapter Nine

I leave Mitzi at her barracks after the meeting, and don't want to be late getting back. I have every intention of telling Mama about Girl Scouts, but I don't want her asking where I've been before I know how I'm going to explain.

A quicker way to get home without using the shortcut that got me into trouble, is hooking a ride with Mr. Ishigo. He drives the coal truck to and from the boiler room near Yama-san's. And today, I'm in luck. He turns the corner, and I flag him down.

"Hi-de-ho there," he says, as I climb into the cab.

Pop would say he's photogenic. "Thank you, Mr. Ishigo."

We bob and lean together in the cab as he avoids ruts and potholes in the dirt road. "Your wife sketches good," I say to be friendly.

He smiles. "She sure does." On a smooth patch, he adds, "Oh, but she's got special permission to sketch, in case you're wondering, but only children and the elderly."

It would make sense that the WRA had rules for sketching. Pop's probably been given special permission to take pictures at Santa Fe. I smile to myself. My father's doing something important there. If someone's sketching and taking pictures, we won't be forgotten.

"Mrs. Ishigo gave me a good idea," I say, and tell him about the peach can label and how I used it to write a letter to my father. "But unfortunately, it's been turned into something else." I show him my origami heart. "See?"

He smiles. "Gosh, Koko. That's real sharp looking." He ticks his head as if he's agreeing with his own happy thought. "Yep. Estelle and I met at art school. I studied acting, and she studied art." He stares ahead, smiling. "It wasn't legal for us to get married here, you know. So we got hitched in Mexico."

I wonder why Uncle Sam would make loving someone illegal. I think Pop should reconsider helping Uncle Sam and come home. The truck hits another pothole, and I change the subject. "I can't draw like your wife, but Mama's going to help me with an Arts and Crafts badge for Girl Scouts."

"No foolin'? Well, you work hard at it and don't be afraid to make a mistake."

A few more bumps and we reach my block. I hop

from the cab. "Thanks, Mr. Ishigo. You've saved me from being late."

He tips his hat and toots the horn goodbye.

I agree with Mrs. Ishigo. I wouldn't have left Mr. Ishigo's side either. Not for a million bucks.

"Hey, kid."

My heart skips a beat. I know the voice.

"You've got some explaining to do."

Turning slowly, I face the MP who almost shot me. "I'm on my way to 24-20," I tell him.

"That's not why I've stopped you."

I think he must eat children for dinner.

"I've been checking around. No one's ever heard of a *Pick-up-Trash* Girl Scout Badge."

It's hard to think when the meanest guard in camp is glaring at you. A piece of tissue used in the beauty parlor flips crosses the ground between us. I step on it, trying to remember the exact name of the badge.

He's waiting.

I pick up the tissue paper, still trying to remember, but the only thing that comes to me is that I still haven't written a new letter to Pop. "Oh, you must've heard me wrong, sir," I say. "I'm pretty sure I told you it was the Community Samaritan Badge." The fib pops out, like that reflex Yama-san talked about. The tissues flutter between my fingers. "You've heard about Mr. Henderson wanting this place cleaned up, haven't you?"

He doesn't move. "Community Samaritan Badge?"

I nod, flushed to my ear tops with bee buzz. *Why is he picking on me?*

His stare narrows. "I'll be checking about that, young lady."

I squint up at him.

He stares. "So?"

"Sir?"

"Thought you were going somewhere."

I spin around. *One, two, three* ... the further away I step, the quieter the buzzing gets. Pretty soon, I want to go back and admit that I knew all along that there's no such thing as a *Pick-up Trash* badge, but my feet won't let me.

Four, five, six ... Mitzi would have been brave enough to tell him, I bet. I wish I could be more like her—honest, good and obedient. *Seven, eight, nine* ... my feet drag out of step with my heart. By the time I've reached the Gamachi's barracks, they're too heavy to lift.

Mrs. Gamachi is outside with her husband. He's sitting in a chair in his stocking feet.

"Where are Mr. Gamachi's shoes?" I ask.

"At the canteen," she grumbles, "repaired and ready to be picked up."

"Well, why don't you get them, then?"

She frowns. "If I could wait in the shoe repair line all day, he'd have them on, now wouldn't he?"

Last week Mr. Gamachi wandered off looking for his son, but he doesn't have one.

"You know he can't wait in line with me," she adds. "And I can't leave him."

"I'll go for you."

Mrs. Gamachi tilts her head like she didn't hear me straight. "What?"

I don't want to run into the MP again, but I don't want Mr. Gamachi to go another day without his shoes. I hold out my hand. "Got the claim ticket?"

She hesitates, but in a flash, she's up her stairs and into her compartment. She returns with a blue ticket. "Are you sure, Koko? I don't want to make you late getting home."

"I'll go lickety-split," I say, and scoot off toward the canteen, ducking, crawling and skipping in line. In a jiffy, I'm saying thank you to the clerk for Mr. Gamachi's boots. Sometimes it's handy being short and pushy.

Mrs. Gamachi's surprised when she sees me return so soon. "Look what Koko has for you, Yushi," she says to her husband. He gives a whiskery grin. He may not recognize his wife all the time, but he recognizes his boots. He holds them in his lap like old friends.

"Thank you, so much, Koko," she says. "I recognize the good work of Moon Rabbit when I see it." She reaches into her apron pocket and places a buffalo nickel into my palm. "Here. An unexpected kindness deserves an unexpected reward."

I wasn't sure what a rabbit or the moon had to do with anything, but I was grateful for the nickel. It's round and solid in my palm—and doing quick arithmetic in my head—it's enough to buy a stamp and envelope for another letter to Pop, with a penny to spare! "Thank you, Mrs. Gamachi."

"You know the legend about Moon Rabbit, don't you?" she asks. "About the monkey, fox, and rabbit that helped a hungry beggar?"

I shake my head.

"Monkey gathered nuts and berries for the beggar to eat. Fox was good at hunting. He caught lots of fish. Rabbit wasn't good at gathering or hunting, but he was most earnest to help the hungry beggar. And then the rabbit surprised them all with an unthinkable act . . ."

"He threw himself into the fire!" spouts Mr. Gamachi, throwing his arms up for emphasis.

Mrs. Gamachi sucks in air, surprised at her husband's participation. "Why, that's right, Yushi."

"But why'd he do that?" I ask. "Didn't it hurt? What about his family?"

"Don't be upset, Koko. The fire sounds like a bad thing, but it's not the end of the rabbit's life, or the story."

"*Ano wa yūkan do,*" says Mr. Gamach.

Mrs. Gamachi turns to her husband. "*Hai*, Yushi. The rabbit was brave." She faces me, smiling. "You see, the beggar wasn't really a beggar. He was a moon god in search of kindness. He whisked the rabbit out of the fire just in time, and in a puff of smoke, took the rabbit back home with him to live in the moon. And to this day, when a full moon appears, you can still see the rabbit there busy making *mochi*, reminding us to be patient and kind."

"And brave," pipes Mr. Gamachi.

My mouth waters for *mochi*, the warm treat of puffed rice celebrated at New Years when we were together as a family. It's the first time, in a long time, that I remember home clearly.

Mrs. Gamachi looks up even though the moon can't be seen yet.

Mr. Gamachi looks up.

I look up.

Though I can't see the moon or Moon Rabbit, I can believe. If a letter can change into a heart, and a rabbit can live on the moon, then I can believe my family will be together again soon.

JU
Chapter Ten

"Yuk. What an awful dinner," Shirley says. "Rice heaped with syrupy peaches?"

I'm up the steps and into 24-20 ahead of Mama and Shirley. Now that I have paper and a nickel, I'm anxious to write my new letter to Pop. "The Vienna sausages weren't as bouncy as usual," I say.

Shirley laughs. "Remember that whacky contest the boys had seeing who could bounce their sausage the highest?"

"Yeah, and then they ate them."

Shirley and I are laughing, laughing together like we used to.

"Do you suppose the other camps have the same awful food?"

"Let's not complain, dear," Mama says, picking up her latest mending project.

"But peaches on top of rice?"

Mama sighs. "They're just thinking it might serve

as a treat, dear, since generally speaking, Japanese like rice and peaches."

"Give me *real* rice, and I might consider it."

"It's better than potatoes all the time," I say. I tuck a piece of bread I saved from dinner into my school bag for the next time I visit Berkeley. The permission slip from Girl Scouts is there. With Mama feeling better, having writing paper now, earning a nickel, and Shirley's good mood, it's the perfect time to bring up the subject of Girl Scouts. "Mama, may I talk with you about something?"

Shirley drowns me out. "Tell me, would the *hakujin* who run this place top their mashed potatoes with peaches? Yuk."

Mama sighs, answering the way she always does, even before Wyoming. "There are lots of hungry people in the world who would be happy to have syrupy rice to eat."

Shirley rolls her eyes, too late to take it back.

Mama crinkles her eyebrows. "With the world at war, do you really want to complain about having sweetness on your plate?"

"Mama, may I talk with you about something? It's important."

Donk-donka-donk-donk. Donk-donk.

Shirley jumps to open the door, and a flicker of a hope stirs inside me that it might be Pop.

"Oh, hi-ee Marty," Shirley says.

Marty Okamoto, Kenny's big brother and the boy

who always teases me, whips off his cap. "Hey, hey, wha'da'ya say, girls. Hello, Half-Pint. Do something different with your hair?"

I swing away from his hand that tries to pat my head. "Keep your mitts to yourself."

"Have you already had dinner, Marty?" Mama asks to be polite.

"Oh, yes ma'am. Me and my pals always eat together at the mess hall." He turns to Shirley. "You can sit with Yuki and me anytime you want."

"Next time, maybe," she answers, as if Mama would allow it. She may sit with her friends on one side of her, but the other side belongs to us.

Marty pulls Mama's footstool up to the table and plops himself down. "Hey, did you hear about the riot at Tule Lake?"

My ears perk up. This must be the trouble the father in line at the post office was talking about yesterday.

Shirley giggles like a stupid-head. "Bet it was over lousy food. I just love slimy, syrupy rice, Marty, don't you?"

"Heck, whatever you don't want, I'll eat."

Mama offers him a cup with a peach she saved from dinner.

"Gee, thanks Mrs. H." He digs in, but I want him to tell us more.

"A riot?" I ask. Mr. Oyama didn't want me to worry, but now I know the reason why. I'm anxious to hear more, and I'm usually never interested in anything Marty says.

"Koko," says Mama. "Let's not talk about something we're not sure is true." I bite the inside of my cheek to keep quiet.

"I bet those Japanese Nationals were behind it," Marty adds, with a mouth of orange mush. "They're probably spies for the Japanese Emperor, Hirohito."

"How's your mother, Marty?" Mama asks to change the subject. "Sorry to hear she took that awful tumble on the ice last month."

Marty swallows peach. "Oh, she's fine, Mrs. H. Thanks for asking." He uses the cup to make a point. "You know, we're lucky here at Heart Mountain. Our hospital is topnotch."

Suddenly, our attention shifts to the shouting from the other side of our wall. It's our neighbor, Mr. Takata. I can't make out the Japanese. Mama understands what's being said, I'm sure, but she would think it rude to repeat a family's private affair.

"What's he saying, Marty?" asks Shirley.

Marty listens for a moment. "The old man's demanding his wife to leave with him for Japan," he whispers. "George and Mickey, too."

Heartache creeps into the room like a fog. George is a high school senior, and Mickey is his six-year-old brother who's always begging him to play catch.

"That's enough," Mama says, slacking in her chair. "We don't need to know people's private business."

Whatever Mrs. Takata says to answer her husband,

it sends him into a rage. We hear his feet stomp across the floor, making our hanging light bulb shimmy from the rafter. I'm worried for George and Mickey.

Marty gulps. "Holy cow. Mrs. Takata has flat out told her husband she's staying in America where her boys were born."

"Why would she want to go back to Japan?" I ask. "She's lived here practically her whole life."

"That's not the point," says Marty. "Japanese wives do what their husbands tell them."

"Not if they're wrong," I say.

"Yes," he says. "Even then."

Shirley crosses her arms. "That's ridiculous."

I mimic her. "Yeah, ridiculous." Remembering what Mama said about us each following our own private rules, Mrs. Takata must be following hers.

George cuts into the argument. "Dad, be reasonable ..." he starts, finishing in Japanese.

Marty looks shocked. "Holy cow. George just told his father he's joined the Army and will be leaving after he graduates."

"*Tsk*," I say. "Why would George leave his family while they're locked up here?"

"Oh, I'd join, too, if I were eighteen. I'd like a chance to fight for my country. Germans, Italians, or Japanese, they're no kin to me, I'm an American."

Something crashes against the wall, and we all jump.

Mrs. Takata's crying, and I feel guilty for eavesdropping. But there's never any privacy for any of us, anywhere in camp.

Marty's face turns white. "Mr. Takata ... has just disowned George for joining the Army."

I shake my head. "Disown?"

Marty stares at the wall. "It means George is dead, Koko." He swallows hard. "Dead to his family. Forever."

"You mean Mr. Takata loves Japan more than his own son?"

Marty leans forward, looking almost gloomy enough for me to start liking him. "But sons get disowned, Koko. Daughters, too." He taps a spot on the table to make his point. "That's why the old Japanese ways have got to go."

We hear a scuffle. Chairs clunk to the floor—and then an awful sound of someone being slapped.

Marty knocks the stool over when he stands. "I've got to find my father. This is a matter for security, and maybe the MPs."

Mama and I look at each other—we don't want to give any reason for the MPs to arrive. "No, Marty, wait," I say.

The floor planks under my feet vibrate as Mr. Takata charges out of his unit door, through the entryway, and down the steps of the barracks. Marty goes to the window.

Shirley follows. "Where's Mr. Takata taking Mickey?" As silly as she sounded before, nervousness is in her voice.

"I don't want to go!" Mickey pleads. "Please, no Papa, no!"

Even from my safe place next to Mama, Mickey's feet kicking and scraping on the ground outside scares me. She holds me as if her arms could shield me from the awful sounds of a family breaking.

Marty answers Shirley with fists clutched. "Anyone who wants to catch a ship back to their precious Japan go to Tule Lake." He puts his cap on. "Too bad for George's little brother. But as far as I'm concerned, anyone who wants to leave, good riddance, including those good for nothing troublemakers, traitors and spies at Santa Fe."

Lightning cracks. Flashes. I look at Mama, expecting her to set Marty straight. But her face is as gray as the ash in our stove.

Family Scene, Estelle Ishigo

JU-ICHI
Chapter Eleven

"All right everyone," says Marty's father. "The excitement's over. Go back to your units."

A red handprint covers one side of George Takata's face. His arm is around his mother who's curled into his side, crying. Lights in the midway reflect the rain falling, but it doesn't stop us from wanting to help, even though we're helpless.

"Sorry to bother everyone," George says, trying to sound steady and mature. "But my mom and I will be fine now."

Mama gently pries his mother from him. "I know, George." She guides Mrs. Takata toward their unit. "Girls, it's starting to pour. Go inside. I'll be there shortly."

Marty follows Shirley. I lag behind. On the ground, with raindrops tapping its small brim, lies Mickey's baseball cap. I slip it into my overalls.

"Need help taking any of your mother's dishes

and trays back to the mess hall?" Marty asks Shirley. "You know, from when she wasn't feeling well and you brought her food?"

"You'd do that for *me*, Marty?" Shirley sing-songs.

I never want to be boy cra-zee. It makes you forget what's important. "You're worried about stupid dishes with what's just happened?" I yell at both of them, throwing my arms up in the air.

"Wouldn't want you guys in hot water over breaking rules, you know."

I gather the few plates, trays, cups and forks belonging to the mess hall and dump them into Marty's arms. "There. We're legal. Now you need to go."

He thinks I'm joking. I push him out our door. "Scram," I say, and close it in his face.

Shirley yanks my arm. "Quit acting like a brat."

I pull away. "Then quit acting like a silly-head. Marty's too old for you."

She puts her hands on her hips. "Who says I want Marty as a boyfriend?"

"*Ohooo, you'd do that for me, Marty?*"

"Shut up, Frog."

"You shut up."

The door opens. "Girls! Haven't we had enough fighting for one night?"

I rub my arm. Shirley's never been rough with me. But that was before the bus ride, train ride and the long walk up the hill.

"How's Mrs. Takata, Mama?" Shirley sets tea cups on the table.

"Resting."

"I can't believe George's father would do that to his family."

This is something I can agree with Shirley on. "Mickey loved playing catch with George. What did he ever do wrong?"

"What has any of us done?" says Shirley.

Mama sits at the table, turning her tea cup in place. "We mustn't judge Mr. Takata too harshly. He's torn between two countries; the one he was born in, and the one he's known most of his life. It's like having to choose between your mother and father."

Making sure Shirley and Mama aren't looking, I slide Mickey's cap under my mattress for safekeeping. "Mrs. Takata broke a rule in not doing what her husband told her to, but I'm proud of her."

Mama adds, "Yes, and we must keep a lookout on ways we can help her."

Shirley pours Mama tea. "Sorry to change the subject, but there's no school tomorrow, so Yuki and I volunteered to help with the big kite contest, okay? Over a hundred kids have signed up."

Distracted, Mama stares at the steam in her cup, like it swirled a secret only she could understand. "Yes, of course. The kite contest."

My school bag is open next to me on my bed, and the permission slip from Girl Scouts peeks out. I don't want to mention it to my mother now. I've just seen how a family can be torn apart by disagreement. But I promised Mitzi, and it's the right thing to do. I drum up nerve and bring the slip to the table.

"What's this?"

Shirley reads over Mama's shoulder. "Uh-oh. Here we go again."

Mama looks over the edge of the slip at me. "I thought we were finished with this subject."

I sit straighter. Clear my throat. If she says no, I'll never mention Girl Scouts again for the rest of my life. "Mitzi invited me."

"So?" says Shirley.

Mama silences her with a look, and then turns to me. "Wearing a pin and sash doesn't make a person a good citizen."

"That's true," Shirley says. "We're good citizens, and look what's happened to us."

Tightness lassos my chest, and it doesn't have anything to do with not knowing what to say to convince her. The truth is, I'd gone to the meeting behind Mama's back knowing how she was against it. It's something I'm adding to my private list of rules. Number 7: Never scheme. My next words spin out like hot coals. "I've already been to the first meeting."

"*Tsk*. See, Mama? Koko just does whatever she pleases. Isn't there a rule or a law in Girl Scouts about obeying, or something?"

Rain taps across the roof. I take in a big breath. "Mr. Henderson will give certain Girl Scouts special passes to leave camp in order to greet the trains stopping at Heart Mountain." My thoughts melt into one good one and my deepest hope spills out. "I want to meet Pop at the train when he comes. I don't want him to feel alone and abandoned, like we did, when he walks up the hill."

Shirley's quiet. "Oh."

The weight on my shoulders seems to lift. It felt good telling Mama what I wanted to do.

Mama gives the slip a good long look. "To be honest," she says, quietly, "sometimes things we've looked at the same way a hundred times needs to be looked at differently." She smiles. "Got a pencil?"

I can't believe it! I throw my arms around her. "Thanks Mama." And then, I hug her some more.

She signs the slip and hands it to me. "Put it in your bag so you don't lose it."

As I tuck it away, I get an idea—something to lift everyone's mood. "How about we all write a letter to Pop?"

"Sure," says Shirley. "But what are we going to write it on, the sky?"

"Nope." I reach inside and hold up the paper Miss Percy gave us for the *American* assignment. "I've got paper."

Mama's face brightens.

I'm happy Mr. Oyama turned my letter into a heart. Pop hearing from all of us will be much better than just hearing from me. Mama and Shirley write short letters, and then it's my turn.

Thursday, April 15, 1943

Dear Pop

I've been good.

I tap my cheek with my pencil, trying to think what kind of truth the WRA will like best.

My friend Mitzi and I visited the new library. And guess what? Mama says I can be a Girl Scout! I have a big surprise, too, but can't tell you. You'll have to get here to see it. The sooner the better. By Mother's Day would be perfect.

I don't want to mention my ride with the MP. Outside, a wolf howls, sounding too close to camp. It reminds me not to mention Berkeley either, or the green and red collar I braided for him with Mama's mending scraps.

Mitzi wants me to help plant a Victory Garden.

I want to tell him about Mama feeling better, but she wouldn't want him to know she was sick in the first place.

I've been taking pictures. Not real ones, of course. It's against WRA rules to take pictures, and we all follow rules around here at 24-20.

Something patriotic might be good.

We're getting a new flag in May. Mr. Henderson is planning a dedication for it. But, you'll be here by then, right?

The whistle sounds for lights out. "Finished?" Mama asks.

I sign my name. Done. Happy. Luck is with me, once again.

Mama folds the finished sheet of paper with our words and slides it into an envelope she must have already had. That saves me two cents out of my nickel. Maybe they'll have Botan rice candies at the canteen.

"It felt good to write to your father."

"And here's a lock of my hair to put with it," Shirley says, stuffing it inside. "For luck."

I'm about to tell Shirley what a great idea it is.

"So don't lose it when you mail it." She adds, "or I'll never forgive you."

Mama places the envelope at her bedside next to Pop's *ticking* pocket watch. "On Saturday I get paid for some mending, so Monday you can buy a stamp at the post office and send it off."

"No need to wait until Monday," I say. "I have a *fortuitous* solution." I dig into my book bag again and hold up the silver, shiny nickel. "I think this will cover it," I feel a grin stretching across my face. "And to think, we owe it all to Mr. Gamachi's shoes."

The sky and wind
were all they had,
sailing on a kite
to greet the clouds
only a string
from glowing sun
down into shadows of night

Kite Flying, Estelle Ishigo

VOL. II No 17   2 Cents Within City 5 Cents Elsewhere

Victory Gardens To be Grown Here

Heart Mountain will soon get their chance at gardening, for according to the agriculture foreman, several acres of the virgin soil on the western end of the project area will be plowed, leveled and later parceled out to those who wish to have victory gardens of their own.

JU-NI
Chapter Twelve

The buffalo nickel and our family letter are in my hand. The air smells so clean it makes my eyes water. It's a beautiful day.

Was a beautiful day.

My not-so-favorite MP stands outside the administration building. He waves me over. My heart gallops. *What now?* Doesn't he have better things to do?

"I've been doing some checking."

My hand covers my mother's writing on the envelope to protect it from his x-ray vision.

"Seems there's no such thing as a Community Samaritan Badge."

I look up at him through bangs. This time, I remember the name of the badge. "Oh, sorry sir, I meant the Community *Safety* Badge. Samaritan and safety sound sort of the same."

He stands as firm as a rock. His face doesn't even

twitch. "And how do you explain that you're not listed as a Girl Scout with any of the troop leaders in camp."

Even though I'm clean as a whistle for fibs, he makes me feel like I'm not. "Well sir . . ." I try to think what Mitzi would say, what she'd do. "Oh sir, you're absolutely correct. I'm so sorry for any misunderstanding."

He gives me a side stare.

The bees are at the tip of my tongue, waiting to attack, but I hold them back. I know he can't read any lies in me today. "Technically, I'm not a Girl Scout until my in-ves-ti-ture."

He puts hands on his hips. "Investiture, huh?" He nods, but I don't think he means yes.

"It's a big deal ceremony for Girl Scouts like they have for soldiers after boot training."

"Boot camp training."

"Isn't that what I said?"

"I'll be checking this *investiture* thing out."

"Yes, sir."

He turns and heads toward the administration building. I don't want to follow even though our family letter is burning in my hand. Someone else I don't want to see joins him, the social welfare lady with clipboard and all. Rule 6: AVOID MPS AND SOCIAL WELFARE LADY. They talk on the steps like two Do Not Enter signs. There's no other way for me to get inside the building except to pass them. The MP casts his two icy blues in my direction, says something, and the lady's gaze follows. There's sudden pounding in my ears. Either I walk up the stairs now—or mail the letter later.

Mitzi rushes up and out of breath. "Come quick."

"Just a minute, Mitz, I'm thinking."

She tugs my sleeve. "But it's an emergency."

An emergency for an emergency might be just what I need. "What kind of emergency?"

"An important one."

I check the stairs. Another MP has joined them and offers a cigarette to the corporal. Standing here will only draw attention to me.

"Well, if it's an emergency, let's go." I stuff the letter and nickel in my overall pocket. By the time I finish with Mitzi's emergency, the MPs and social welfare lady will be gone. And, I have plenty of time before the three o'clock deadline.

Mitzi takes me around the corner on the other side of the building. "It's about my father's garden."

Tsk. "That's your emergency? Boy, you really want that Gardener Badge."

"*Our* Gardener Badge. Wait until you hear what Mr. Henderson gave father permission to do."

She's hardly finished her sentence when her father approaches. "Good morning, Koko. Mitzi tells me you're going to help with the garden." His dash-dash mustache raises in a smile, and I can't help smiling back. "Come on, let me show you where it's going to be. The best view is a little bit of a walk, though."

We pass the teeter-totters and swing sets and the apartments of WRA staff. A cocker spaniel plays with children in a fenced yard. Only the WRA people are allowed to have pets. I wonder when Berkeley will be old enough to play fetch, and then worry when he will, because he's grown big and fat in just two weeks.

We pass the mud hole, which was our skating rink during the winter. There's talk it'll be our swimming hole this summer. We pass the motor pool area, and walk closer to the fence.

"I've never been this close to the barbwire," Mitzi whispers. "Isn't it exciting?"

I'm glad she can't read minds.

We reach Gate 7 and Mr. Sakada shows an official paper to the MP. He waves us on with the butt of his rifle. We reach the fence and stop.

Mr. Sakada points across the road. "Starting from that tree line, girls, and from the Shoshone River all the way to the road, is where Mr. Henderson says we can plant a garden. It's a thousand acres."

I give a dry whistle.

"Just imagine rows of peas and cantaloupe and carrots," he adds, offering Mitzi and I a look through his binoculars. "Hundreds of people in the camp have volunteered to help plant and drive tractors. Over there's a pipeline. We're going to finish it and bring water from the river."

The wind spins brown dirt over the chunky land of sage brush and rock. I remember Yama-san seeing the gushing, chocolate-colored river from his roof.

"It's the camp's Victory Garden," says Mitzi, "like the gardens all over the country being grown to support the war effort."

I look over at Mitzi. She'd never admit it, but even with river water, there's no way in a million years a garden could grow in all that dead dirt. So, not wanting to sound like an old fuddy-duddy, I turn to Mr. Sakada. "This is a very nice project, sir."

Squeals of laughter rise from the big field behind us. Early kite flyers gather for the contest that Shirley mentioned. Ruth Niwa hollers, "Hey, Mitzi! Over here!"

"Oh father, please, may we go?" She clasps her hands like she's praying. "Please?"

"I promised your mother I'd bring you right back to help with *Obaachan*."

"And I've got an important letter to mail," I say.

She faces me with her back to her father. "But we have lots of time before the post office closes, right?" Her mouth twists and contorts into a silent, pleading, p-l-e-a-s-e.

I've never known my friend *not* to want to take care of her grandmother. Or *not* want to please her father. I can't bear her looking so miserable. "Mr. Sakada? I remember my sister saying they needed help with the little kids, today, and Mitzi's a great helper."

The old me feels perfectly fine in stretching the truth a little. But the new me is queasy. He wavers. The pleasant day and the promise of kite flying has lured everyone out of their barracks—kids with homemade kites, parents, grandparents, teachers and friends. It's like a parade. Cotton shirts and brightly colored kimonos have replaced coats. Shoes and socks have replaced muddy boots. Toddlers run barefoot.

"It's too nice of a day to say no," he says.

Mitzi squeals and hugs her father. "Oh, thank you, father." She locks elbows with me. "We'll be great helpers together, Koko."

"I just need to get back in time to mail my letter."

"You will. I promise, you will."

The first kite flyers up were the first- and second-graders. Mitzi and I sweat and laugh, running to help lift kites. Shirley even smiles and waves when she sees me, and I'm reminded of what I need to do. "I'll be right back, Mitzi. I'm going to mail my letter."

"But the third-graders from Block 5 are lining up now, and you're the best at fixing tails."

It would mean another hour, but I have time. "Okay."

The wind is perfect. Kites are flying high. I frame the shot and snap. The day is back to being beautiful.

Not so beautiful.

I pinch the outside pocket of my overalls, expecting a crinkle from the envelope, but my hand pushes through a hole instead. A big hole. One that I forgot to ask Mama to fix. "It's gone."

"What's gone?"

I check and recheck my other pockets. "My letter. That's what's gone."

"The one you were going to mail?"

I'm numb at first, until panic sets in. It zaps through my body as I frantically check the ground, under my feet, behind me. My mind and heart are racing, but I can't breathe. I narrow my gaze at Mitzi, and then the words slip out like it's someone else speaking. "How could you?"

"How could I what?" Mitzi's brows wrinkle in confusion.

"You told me it was an emergency, and now my letter's gone."

Her face puckers. Her lip trembles. "I'm, I'm sorry."

I watch tears slide down her cheeks, and it's like a cold bucket of water has just been poured over my head.

I'm a terrible friend.

She gotta good eye. Yama-san would tell me, *shikata ga nai,* losing the letter couldn't be helped. But it doesn't match what I'm feeling. Rule 4: Pay Attention. I could have prevented this, should've stayed focused, and then the letter wouldn't have been lost, and Mitzi wouldn't be crying. I take her hand. "It's my fault. I should've finished doing what I was supposed to do."

Mitzi and I apologize to each other a hundred times as we retrace our steps. For an hour we zigzag back and forth, back and forth, across the field where we'd been running—nothing.

We search the ground all the way back to the administration building to find a big sign tacked on the door:

Do Not Disturb—WRA Meeting in Progress.

"Sorry," Mitzi says for the hundredth time. "But you can always write another letter tomorrow, right?"

I raise my arm to hide my face. Mitzi's my friend, my best friend, but she doesn't know about riots, last trucks to Santa Fe, last nickels, or what happens on the other side of the fence. She only knows the goodness of her father's hope for a Victory Garden.

The nickel and envelope—Shirley's lock of hair—are lost, swooped up and swallowed by Wyoming wind. It's a sign.

A terrible sign.

Our family will never be together again.

JU-SAN
Chapter Thirteen

Heart Mountain sprouts veins of green down its sides. The sun shines warm every day. People are happy that spring has arrived.

Not me.

Spring has left my father behind.

Mama and Shirley don't know that I've lost our family letter. I'm working up courage to hear Mama's disappointment in her voice, or Shirley's full attack of frog names. The idea of letting them down again hangs like a winter wool coat on my heart.

"No, Koko. No letter from your father, today," Mr. Oyama tells me this morning. "Trucks are running again. You'll hear soon, I'm sure."

But losing the letter is not a lucky sign.

I'm giving up on signs.

Clouds of dirt pucker and rise from the many tractors plowing the Victory Garden, making everyone in camp cough and sneeze. Smoke from burning sagebrush drifts into camp almost smelling like Mrs. Takata's Japanese incense. Hundreds of people are helping to prepare land for planting, even The Pioneers.

The Pioneers is our new Girl Scout troop name, and we've grown to ten members. At least Mama let me join Girl Scouts. It sidetracks me from the homesickness none of us mention but always feel.

Today The Pioneers are working on our gardener badge and stomping clumps of dirt left by tractors to make it easy for seeds to grow. I'm stomping with extra zest. *Stomp, stomp, stomp.* A train greeter should be diligent, and I want to do the best I can since luck's not on my side. But deep down, a little spark of *gaman* reminds me to be patient. *Patient.* Pop's got to be on his way.

The little spark didn't last long. After a full day of stomping, Mrs. Somekawa announces that only one girl from each troop in camp will be selected for train greeter duty. My chances have been cut in half. I'm going to work twice as hard.

I volunteer to help Mr. Sakada plant extra rows of cucumber. A train greeter should be willing to go above and beyond the call of duty.

Ruth's an eager beaver, too. "I planted extra rows of squash today, Mrs. Somekawa."

At our last meeting, I showed Miss Makabe the progress I've made on my quilt scene for the Arts and Crafts badge. I think a train greeter should be persistent.

Ruth's persistent, too. "My paints for my project

are special ordered from Montgomery Ward."

Today, Miss Makabe makes an announcement. "Next week you'll be working toward your Community Safety Badge. Mr. Henderson wants the camp looking nice for Easter Sunday."

My heart leaps. I'm the best at finding trash.

"Oh, I've been collecting trash around my barracks for weeks," Ruth brags.

My face must show my disappointment. Becoming a Girl Scout is hard enough—but being the best so I can be a train greeter feels impossible.

"Don't worry, Koko," says Mitzi. "If I'm chosen as train greeter, I'll give it to you. Your dad will be coming soon, and I want you to be there to greet him."

Camp Cleaning, Estelle Ishigo

"Ah, geez, Mitz." I hug her. A good friend knows just what to say.

The next week, everyone in camp is sweeping,

dusting and scrubbing. Dressed in old pants and shirts, we all head up the knoll to the hospital. We're excited about adding another patch to our sashes with the Community Safety Badge.

Not me.

A good Girl Scout would have told their mother and sister about losing an important letter. I can't even look them in the eye.

Mrs. Somekawa assigns us our sections to be cleaned up: Down First Street to Avenue G to Central to the hospital. "Mitzi and Koko, you have the area around the hospital."

"I'll cover the entrance area," Mitzi says. "You take the side down to the back steps."

I wince. "I think I saw rats around there."

"There won't be any rats."

"Rats bite, you know, and they're all over the place since it's been warmer."

"I bet you a million bucks you won't spot a single rat."

"With my luck lately, bet I do."

She shrugs. "We can switch if you want."

I take a big breath. "Just kidding."

With a stick I found, I poke an old shoe stuck in the dirt, whack a woodpile for an old hat lodged underneath, and flip over a piece of tarpaper. No rats. I'm sweating under my shirt, but I'm almost done. Only one area is left to check. The dreaded steps.

Down the side of the building toward the boiler

room I hesitate. A cardboard box sits on the steps, wiggling. Rats!

Goose bumps prickle down my back and I'm ready to run. But a train greeter should be diligent, persistent, and go beyond the call of duty. I give the box a poke. It wiggles again.

I run.

Ah-choo.

Do rats sneeze? With stick raised, I peek over the box's edge to find a chubby-cheeked face smiling up at me.

A baby.

I blink twice to make sure I'm not imagining things.

Yep. It's a baby.

Questions whiz through my mind. "Hello there," I whisper. "Where's your mama? Are you all right?" She squirms inside her pink cocoon of a blanket, her face puckering like she's on the verge of crying. I rush to pick her up and hold her tight. She's lighter than I expect, lighter than a thousand perfect wishes bundled in pink. Yama-san said babies bring promises of a better future.

Holding her makes it feel like it's true.

A baby's a sign—a wonderful sign—that even when things seem impossible to get better, they can. Puffs of her breath hit my cheek. "Don't worry, Baby. You're safe now." She wraps her teeny fist tight around my pinky finger, and it might as well be my heart. I walk carefully to show Mitzi. "A baby? You found a baby, Koko?"

I step extra careful as we walk to where The Pioneers are gathering. Mrs. Somekawa wipes her hands on her khaki-colored skirt before lifting Baby from my arms, her little fist never letting go of my finger.

Miss Makabe leans over her sister's shoulder and makes smooching noises.

Mrs. Somekawa is teary-eyed. "Poor little girl." Most of the Pioneers are teary-eyed, too. We hover over her, *oohing* and *aahing*.

Ruth wrinkles her nose. "She smells."

Mitzi wiggles Baby's foot. "Where's your family, little girl?"

"Why, we're her family now," I say, echoing exactly what I said to Berkeley.

"Yeah, her family," echoes Millie and Fusa.

"No, we're not," says Ruth.

Mrs. Somekawa pats Baby's bottom as she rocks her. "Baby's an innocent person in this awful war and deserves a family. It's a good thing Koko found her."

"Well, then it's also a good thing we have a social welfare department," Ruth says. "Because children without a mother and father get fostered out."

Mitzi rolls her eyes. "Oh, Ruthie, don't be like that."

"Like what?"

"Acting like you don't care when we all know you do."

"Let's take her inside," says Mrs. Somekawa, whisking away a tear. "The nurse will need to check her out."

Ruth whispers meanly in my ear. "Finding that baby doesn't mean you'll be the train greeter from our troop."

I feel too floaty to have her words take hold of me. "My Community Safety Badge will be my favorite badge of all," I announce to everyone. "It'll always remind me of you guys, Baby, and that things can get better, even here."

"Yeeeaaah," the girls chime.

久 久 久

The hospital is built with barracks joined to the left, the right, and end-to-end with waiting rooms, nurses' stations, and operating rooms. It smells of iodine and alcohol like Mama's medicine chest back home. One wing for the really sick and contagious people is off limits. Nurse Kirk is in charge of new patients, and Baby's her newest.

I uncurl Baby's fingers from mine, and when I do, I miss their warmth. "Be a good girl. We'll visit soon." One by one, a crowd of nurses take turns holding Baby, *oohing* and *aahing* just like we did.

"Come away, girls," Mrs. Somekawa says. "We've done all we can for now." Miss Makabe suggests we tour the other wings of the hospital while we're here, in case we want to do a First Aid badge. But I know she's doing it on purpose so Baby can rest.

"What kind of mother or father would leave their kid behind?" Ruth says as we walk away. "Right Koko?

You would know, since your father's done the same thing to you."

I gasp. Her words smack the air with a twinge of truth.

"Ruth Niwa!" scolds Mitzi. "Why are you being so mean? You sound like one of those *hakujins* who says hateful things to us for no reason. No matter how many silk flags your mother can buy, you're still stuck here like the rest of us, so be nice." She pulls me away from Ruth so fast, I almost tumble. "Don't listen to her, Koko."

If not for Mitzi, I would cry. Ruth's words match a doubting whisper in my thoughts. What's taking Pop so long? *Has he forgotten us?*"

Mitzi loops her arm through mine as we walk. "Ruth's just jealous."

"Jealous?"

"Because everyone likes you. Even a baby who's just a few days old loves you."

I wonder if Mitzi knows that her smile feels like sunshine. "No, I think she was just glad to get out of that box."

She gives my arm a squeeze. You're the bravest person I've ever met in the whole wide world." She tucks a stray curl behind her ear. "I would just die if my father wasn't with me here in camp."

My steps lighten. "Everyone in camp is brave, Mitzi. They just don't know it yet." But down the hall, someone I don't want to see is standing with Miss Makabe at the nurses' station.

"Koko?" Miss Makabe calls. "Would you join us please?"

I snap against a wall as if it can hide me.

Mitzi's confused. "What's the matter?"

I glance down the hall. "*She's* the matter."

Mitzi looks. "But it's just the social worker."

"She's not exactly the person I want to see to right now."

Mitzi tilts her head, thinking. "Oh, you mean because of what Ruth said?"

"Koko?" calls Miss Makabe again. "Did you hear me?"

My heartbeat quickens. I'm weak at the knees.

"C'mon, I'll go with you."

"Me too. There's safety in numbers."

Mitzi and I snap a glance behind us. It's Ruth.

"Don't look so surprised," she adds, stepping closer. She looks down, and then takes a big breath. "Mitzi's right, Koko. We're all in this together, and I've been a mean jerk. I'm sorry for what I said about your father, and if you need help now, I'm with you."

My heartbeat slows. My knees stop trembling. Steeling my nerve, I push off the wall. "No, but thanks. I need to do this myself."

Nurse Kirk introduces me to the woman who carries trouble on a clipboard. "Koko, I'd like you to meet the lady in charge of social welfare services, Miss Frayne."

Miss Frayne keeps a stern stare on me, and her bun is so tightly pulled up that the corners of her eyes are lifted. "Does this girl speak English?"

Her voice is as tight as her bun. *Of course I do, silly.*

"Of course she does," Miss Makabe answers, placing a hand on my back. "It's okay, Koko. Miss Frayne just has a few things to ask since you're the one who found Baby."

As I answer Miss Frayne's questions, I'm less nervous. She nods to my answers without much comment, until her last one. "You look familiar. Have we met?"

"Oh no, ma'am." I stretch my smile until it feels like a rubber band ready to snap. "But that's okay. We all look the same around here, right?"

She tilts her head with a questioning look.

And, as if three shaky fingers could protect my family, I raise my hand in a salute. "Scout's honor."

JU-YON
Chapter Fourteen

The flagpole is still without its flag this morning. Not for long. The new flag ceremony is next week, which means my American assignment will be due.

Inside the administration building is a mixed crowd standing between me and a possible letter from Pop. I recognize people from inside our camp, but there are also grumpy farmers and ranchers from outside the camp that I've never seen before. I follow along the wall and stand on a chair to catch Mr. Oyama's attention. He sees me and frowns.

No letter from Pop.

I have to will my feet to move from the chair. Forty-two days have gone by since the first day of spring when Pop said he might come.

"Now I'm not going to argue with you people," shouts Mr. Henderson. "We've strived to make this internment camp a smooth running, orderly and progressive city. But it seems your neighbors in Cody and Powell have passed resolutions to keep our people from coming into their towns."

Curious, I push forward to hear more.

"The only way to remedy this situation is for me to cease issuing special passes for anyone to leave camp. And I mean anyone. That means no high school playoffs with the locals, or picnics on Sunday. I'm not even allowing *Sentinel* staff to leave to print our newspaper in Cody. No more passes for anyone who wants to shop in town."

Voices rise. People shuffle. My insides begin to wring me out of breath. "But what about the special passes for train greeters?" I ask, as loud as I can.

"Surely we're not stopping work on the garden?" I recognize Mr. Sakada's voice. "The growing season is already too short."

"Sorry Harry," answers Mr. Henderson. "No one can leave to run their tractors and tillers for the garden. I intend to abide by the wishes of the local town councils."

"You don't mean those in camp who work the beet farms, right?" another man shouts.

"Them, too. No passes. If the farms are in Park County, the towns will have to figure out which citizens want to work those beet farms without our people's help. A farmer wearing a cowboy hat spouts, "Well that's just plain ludicrous." He doesn't notice he's stepping on my boot. "It's too late to hire help from the South."

The men fidget as I pry my way through a forest of legs, but I'm knocked backward.

"Is this because they're angry that so many of our boys are getting killed by the Japanese in the Pacific?" someone asks.

"But don't they understand that most of us in camp are Americans, too, and want to fight?" The pleading in the young man's voice makes it hard for me to swallow.

I'm bumped. Pushed. Hate sprinkles on me as if it was raining stones. I cover my face to protect myself.

"Koko?" It's Mr. Oyama's voice. "Stand aside," he says gruffly to the men. He lifts me, carries me away, but my hands don't leave my face.

"I just want to be a train greeter," I mumble into my palms. He sets me down. We're behind the post office counter, where thousands of letters have been sent and thousands received since Christmas, but none from my father.

"Everything will be all right."

His words are as hollow as Mama's. The ones she never says anymore.

"Feeling better?"

"Why do people think we'd hurt them, Mr. Oyama?"

"You wouldn't. That's why we're all here at Heart Mountain—at all the camps—to prove we would never hurt our fellow Americans."

I sniffle. "It sure is taking a long time for them to get the message."

"*Gaman*, Koko. Patience."

He echoes my father's words written to me over a year ago, before we left home, left Pomona, before our walk up the hill.

"I have something for you," he says. He reaches behind the counter and presents me with an origami crane. With his fingertips placed inside folds on the bottom, he pumps its wings like it's flying. He holds it out to me. "Fold a thousand paper cranes and you'll be granted a wish."

"Thank you, sir."

I've learned in camp that the number eight, a cat with three colors, a rabbit in the moon, and now a thousand paper cranes can help your life.

I just want one letter.

Mr. Henderson bellows from across the room. "This has been discussed long enough, people. Now, go on home, you're dismissed!"

I'm at the door as the group of angry men leave.

"Hey, watch where you're going, kid." It's the cowboy hat man.

My not-so-favorite MP holds the door open, but this time it's not me he's glaring at. "Let the girl through," he tells the man. Cool air rushes in, too wintry for spring.

The toe-stepper exaggerates a loud, impatient sigh. "We'll die of frostbite waiting for her."

Courage roots in my feet. I hold the crane up and pump its wings in front of him like it's flying. "*Gaman*, mister. Patience," and I step away, liking the sound of my boot heels marching off the porch.

STATEMENT OF UNITED STATES CITIZEN OF JAPANESE ANCESTRY

27. Are you willing to serve in the armed forces of the United States on combat duty, wherever ordered? _____ (Yes/No)

28. Will you sear unqualified allegiance to the United States of America and faithfully defend the United States from any or all attack by foreign or domestic forces, and forswear any form of allegiance or obedience to the Japanese emperor, or any other foreign government, power, or organization?

_____   _____
   Date)   (Signature)

NOTE.—Any person who knowingly and willfully falsifies or conceals a material fact or makes a false or fraudulent statement or representation in any matter within jurisdiction of any department or agency of the United States is liable to a fine of not more than $10,000 or 10 years' imprisonment, or both.

JU-GO
Chapter Fifteen

"Lose track of time again?" Shirley has her hands on her hips. "Marty and Yuki are waiting for me."

"Sorry I'm a little late."

"*Tsk*, there you go again with the sorry routine."

Mama's sitting at the table. "What's important is that Koko's here now. Go ahead and meet up with your friends, Shirley. I know you're looking forward to your outing."

"What outing?" I ask.

"Our class is looking for arrowheads on Heart Mountain today."

"I don't think so."

"Oh yes we are. We have special passes."

"Doesn't matter. Mr. Henderson closed the gates this morning. No one can leave, passes or no passes."

Mama stops folding laundry. "What do you mean no one can leave?"

I tell them about what I heard at the administration building and how upset everyone was. "That's why I was late," I add.

Shirley drops her shoulders. "But our class waited three weeks for those passes."

"Sorry."

She plops into her chair at the table. "Stop saying sorry when you're not, Koko."

I sit across from her. "If it helps, it means no passes for train greeters, either."

She crooks her lip. "Yeah, but me hunting arrowheads was something real, Koko. You being a train greeter isn't."

I'm adding *mean* to my list on Shirley: Grouchy, bossy, moody, and *mean*. "What's your beef with me, Shirley? I wasn't the one who said you couldn't hunt for arrowheads."

"Your sister's right, Shirley. That was a mean thing to say. Now, let's leave before we miss breakfast."

Shirley hates to be told by her mother that her sister is right, just like me.

"Mama, I'm just pointing out that if Koko's still saying sorry all the time, it doesn't sound very honest. And if you say she's so much better about following rules, why doesn't she follow the Girl Scout rule about honesty?"

"I'm honest."

"Really?" Shirley's stare has me worried. "Then what about our family letter to Pop?"

The day of the kite contest zaps back to me like lightening: Sun shining—Mitzi's emergency—and our letter gone forever.

Shirley turns to Mama. "Mitzi's mother filled everyone in at the laundry tubs the other day, going on about how broken up Koko was in losing it." She glares at me. "But I guess you weren't broken up enough to tell us, huh?"

Mama sits, pinching the bridge of her nose. "I know about the lost letter."

Shirley sits up as straight as a stick. "You knew?"

"I didn't want you upset. You both were getting along so nicely."

"Koko loses Pop's letter . . . my lock of hair . . . and it's okay Koko doesn't tell us?"

I parrot Mama's excuse, hoping it'll work as my own. "I didn't tell because I didn't want you and Mama upset."

"Not telling is the same as lying, Koko, and I bet Mama doesn't know the *other* things you haven't been honest about."

From the look on my sister's face, I know what's coming.

"Like skipping school."

My cheeks pop hot with embarrassment and anger. "That was a long time ago."

"Last month is not a long time."

Mama sighs. "I know about Koko missing school, too."

Shirley freezes.

I freeze.

Not even a pin drops in the silence, which means anyone in the barracks who's not at breakfast hears, too. A family's business was everybody's business at Barracks 24-20.

"All this time—" Shirley huffs. "How come I'm the last to know anything?" Her face darkens. "Why do I have to overhear terrible gossip about my family at the laundry? It's not like I can avoid it. The toilets are right there."

"What terrible gossip?" Mama asks.

"You know." Shirley lassos the air with her hand. "About things happening around here that people pretend are okay when it's not. Did you know a little old man got shot dead outside the fence at one of the other camps because he was chasing after a dog—a dog! Or that boys are fighting in the alleys over a stupid questionnaire about who's a loyal citizen and who's not? Things are happening that scare me, but it scares me more when it's about my own family."

"Your sister skipping those early days of a cold, drafty classroom isn't the same thing."

Shirley's voice lowers. "I'm not talking about her skipping school, anymore—I'm talking about something worse. Something I should have been told about a long time ago."

Mama turns that ash color that I remember from

the night of the Takata family's argument. "Something worse?"

Shirley sits facing our mother. "Yes. The truth about the *arrest*."

Another zap of memory hits me: The day the MP caught me outside the fence.

"Those gossips told you . . . about the arrest?"

"Yes, Mama."

"About . . . about your father . . . your father being arrested?"

All the air in the room falls to the floor, and it's suddenly hard for me to breathe.

JU-ROKU
Chapter Sixteen

"I was talking about Koko," Shirley whispers, ready to cry. "They said Koko got arrested by an MP."

Mama's face is as still as a picture. I want her to hurry up and explain, but I'm afraid of what I'll hear.

"Detained, dear. Not arrested. Your father's been detained at Camp Santa Fe, along with other Japanese, Germans and Italians thought to be spying against the United States."

I move closer to Shirley, waiting, waiting for something that I'm not sure we're ready to hear. If Pop's a spy, it would explain his long absence, no letters, and why Mama got so sick. She's been holding in a terrible secret.

"I'm sorry. I should've told you girls sooner . . ." Her voice is low and serious. "I lied about your father volunteering to go there." She sighs. "It seemed the right thing to do at the time."

Mama fiddles with a fraying edge of her dress and

takes a deep breath. "The night of December 7th, the FBI was arresting people all along the coast . . . looking for anyone on its 'list'—fishermen, salesmen, teachers—who could be spying for the Japanese Emperor. A week later, they came pounding on our door while you girls were at school and demanded to search our apartment. Your father asked if they had a warrant, that as a citizen he had the right to know what he was being charged with. It only made them more determined." Mama blots tears. "He was so brave, girls . . . I never knew your gentle father was so brave."

Shirley's chest heaves as she cries, trying to gulp in enough air to breathe. I squeeze her shoulder, remembering when my school wouldn't let the new Portuguese family's children attend because they didn't speak English. Pop stood up in the meeting. "I'll teach them," he'd said so firmly that no one argued. Most everyone in town appreciated Pop for standing up for what was right.

Mama's cough crackles in her chest as if the words had been stuck there too long. "They said his pictures of the ocean coastline, his frequent trips to Sacramento, and that he went to school in Japan when he was young was proof enough he was spying for Japan. They tore through our apartment and your father's studio. They threw his cameras and pictures—his life's work—into the trunk of their car like it was junk." She waves trembling fingers through the air. "They handcuffed him, put him into their car and drove away, leaving our home in shambles."

"But nothing was messy when we got home," I say,

as if having a tidy house proves your life is in order.

"I straightened up the house before you returned and packed some of your father's things as he so often did when he had an assignment out of town."

"All this time," Shirley says, quietly, "you've kept this from us?"

"We thought he'd be back in a day or two."

It was making more sense to me why the FBI came to our school. "I thought we were getting special treatment because of Pop."

"Yeah," says Shirley. "We were special, all right."

"Every day I kept expecting him to return, especially after his letters started coming. But you see, Santa Fe is different from our camp. It's a prison that's run by the Department of Justice, which means your father's being interrogated every day until he convinces them of his innocence. I feared the worst when his letters stopped. I didn't want to frighten you."

"It might have scared Koko," says Shirley, "but you should've told me. I'm older."

"Who me? I wouldn't have been scared. What was scary was when Mama got sick."

Color is starting to return to Mama's face. "And you see, I'm better now, and it's because of you both." She reaches across the table to take both our hands. "Your father will be so proud of you. I just know he'll be released soon."

Shirley slowly takes her hand back. "Not if they've proven he's a traitor."

"How can you even think that, Shirley?" I ask.

"It doesn't matter what I think, now does it?" She crosses her arms. "So, what's the real truth, Mama. Is he, or isn't he a traitor?"

I close my eyes. What I hear next will be the most important moment of my life.

"Of course your father's not a traitor. Far from it."

Shirley and I breathe easier at the same time.

"He's standing up for his rights, and unfortunately by doing that, it looks like he's a troublemaker." She breathes in deeply. "I'm relieved you girls know the truth. It's been hard for you, but your father is standing firm for all of us by showing the government that as an American—like most of us here in camp—he's been denied the right to due process of law."

"I don't know what that means," I say.

"It means we've been judged without a trial," pipes Shirley. "And since Pop's been gone so long, chances are, they're never going to release him."

There's achy truth in her words. Pop couldn't have kept his promise to join us by spring—he only hoped he could.

Pop, like Moon Rabbit, had thrown himself into the fire.

JU-SHICHI
Chapter Seventeen

April has marched into May. The citizens, businessmen, and farmers of Powell City and Cody banned together against their own resolutions. Mr. Henderson's issuing passes again. Everyone is going about their business as if nothing's wrong. But learning the truth about Pop is like being pushed off a swing before you're ready. Except Shirley and I aren't laughing.

Train greeters will get passes, too, but I've given up on being one. Mitzi's perfect for the job, and Ruth's worked pretty hard, too. Plus, Pop probably won't be on any train soon for me to greet.

Mr. Henderson has opened the west gate on Sundays for climbs up the mountain and family picnics. The camp looks spruced up with flags and flowers on porches, curtains waving in open windows, and gardens cropping up outside people's barracks—flower gardens, rock gardens, and even gardens without a single thing in them except curvy lines raked in the dirt.

It's a pretty picture.

But I'm not snapping any shots.

We're still prisoners, just the same. Like Pop.

And now the boys of the *yes-yes* and *no-no* mothers are so angry with each other, anyone who won't answer yes-yes for numbers 27 and 28 on the loyalty questionnaire are called troublemakers.

Since learning the truth about Pop, we don't talk about it. Shirley keeps the fire burning. I keep counting my steps to the post office, and Mama hums as she mends. Today she's stitching red knots on a white piece of rice sack from the mess hall. She loops and glides her needle a certain way to make each knot perfect.

"May I stitch some of the knots, Mama? It'll be good practice for my Arts and Crafts badge. I'll have five badges in time for the Investiture Ceremony after Mother's Day, and I'm only a few stitches short of finishing my quilt scene."

"I'm sorry, Koko, but these are special sashes that the boys of the 442nd will be wearing as good luck when they leave for war. And the custom calls for only the women born in the zodiac year *tiger* to make the knots."

"You're a tiger?"

She lifts her head from her work. "Yes. Surprised? I'm supposed to stitch as many knots as my age and then pass it on to the next lady on the list. It'll be done when there are a thousand knots stitched to the sash."

"A thousand?" I try to whistle, but it mostly comes out air. I run my fingers over a bumpy section of knots. "What animal am I?"

"You were born the year of the monkey."

I picture myself dangling from a tree limb eating a banana. "They're silly and get into trouble."

"Monkeys are clever and solve difficult problems with ease."

I sigh. "I don't think I'm good at that, otherwise I'd figure out how to get Pop home. What animal is he?"

"Ox. They're not only patient, they're good at inspiring others."

"Like doing what he thinks is right."

Mama brushes a speck of thread from the sash. "There. Finished."

"May I take the sash over to the next tiger lady?"

She chuckles, but a cough catches a ride out with it. "That would be Mrs. Kanabi over on Block 28. Are you sure you want to walk that far?"

"Sure. I have some cans for Yama-san anyway."

She wraps the sash in another cloth and hands it to me. "You should know, this sash is for George. He'll be leaving for training soon."

"Oh." The sash tingles in my hand, and I press my best and warmest feelings into it. It would've been nice to meet George's train after boot camp training. "I've got one more question before I go. What animal is Shirley?"

"A sheep. They're passionate about what they believe in."

I head for the door. "Oh, she's passionate, all right. She's nuts about Marty."

久 久 久

Berkeley jumps at my legs, tugs on my loafers, and jabs his paws into my tummy when I lay on the floor. He licks my face with his scratchy tongue. "Hey boy, do you think my face is a licking toy?"

"Better you than me," says Yama-san. "My face is clean enough."

Berkeley tries to bite at the collar I made for him. He's growing so fat he'll need another one soon. He falls backward and rolls. He runs in crazy circles, pushes off Yama-san's cot and then rolls some more. My sides hurt from laughing when he scoots between my legs, scared by the crash of the cow skull when he knocks it off its shelf.

"Yama-san, what are you going to do when Berkeley scampers after you down the midway?"

He shakes his head. "Guards are too busy breaking up the fights between the *yes-yes* and *no-no* boys to be bothered with a cute puppy. Don't worry."

I'm worried, anyway.

Yama-san draws his lips into a funny pucker. "Okay," he puffs out air. "Don't worry because it's already happened."

My eyes widen.

"Like I said," adds Yama-san. "Berkeley's a very

good secret weapon that makes people forget to fight."

I release my breath. "They let him go?"

"Berkeley's freer than you or me, Koko. No rules for stray dogs, yes? Only stray people."

It was true. More dogs from neighboring farms and towns have strayed into camp. Mrs. Ishigo has at least two that wag after her as she sketches.

The bell for dinner rings. He waves me to follow him. "I have something to show you. Another secret weapon."

Yama-san takes me a different way, and as usual, begins his sky-talk.

haru no umi
I repeat: "har-oo noh oo-me"
the sea at springtime

hinemosu notari
"heen-eh-moh-soo noh-tar-ee"
all day it rises and falls

notari kana
"noh-tar-ee kah-na"
yes, rises and falls."

"Veerry good, Koko. You sound Japanese."

"I am Japanese, Yama-san. Japanese-American."

Yama-san stops at one of the boiler rooms. Moist, hot air hits my face when he opens the door. I haven't seen so much green in one place since leaving Clarksburg. Stacked like books on shelves are hundreds of the shiny tin cans with little green sprouts sticking up. "These are vegetables for Victory Garden," he says.

"Wow, Mitzi will be so excited to tell her father."

He nods his head. "Ah, yes. Mitzi's a good girl."

A question sparks through me, a question I didn't even know I had. We close up the boiler room and finish our walk to mess hall. The midway becomes crowded, slowing our pace. I take a big breath. "Yama-san? Am I good, like Mitzi?"

He chuckles, shakes his head, as if I've told a joke. "No, Koko. You're not good like Mitzi."

Suddenly, my bones feel too heavy to lift.

People in the midway grumble that I'm in their way. Yama-san looks for me when he realizes I'm not following. "*Ashee.*" He guides me out of the midway to stand near someone's rock garden. "*Suggoku gomen nasai*," he says. "So, so sorry, Koko-san. *Gomen nasai.* That came out all wrong." He sits on a big rock and sighs. "What I meant was, Mitzi's good. She does what other people expect."

"But it's exactly what I've been trying to do for two months."

He pulls on his whiskers. "What I mean is . . . you don't do what people expect you to do."

I look at my hands, as if they could explain my confusion. "I don't understand, Yama-san. If *not* doing what people expect is so good, then why was I getting into trouble?"

He leans forward, resting his hands on his knees. "You do what is right, Koko—from here." He softly taps his chest. "That better than good, yes? Better than just obey. *Hai?*"

Understanding soaks into me like ink on paper: slow and permanent. "You mean, just be myself and do the right thing?"

He rests a hand on my shoulder. "I'm proud of you Koko." His eyes blink with shine. "Proud like a grandfather."

I wrap my arms around him and feel his awkwardness in being hugged. I hold tight, as if he's my real *ojiisan*, all solid and good, like roots of a mountain.

JU-HACHI
Chapter Eighteen

Shirley and I are treating Mama for Mother's Day by doing the laundry and letting her sleep. Her cough has been keeping her up at night. I scrub and rinse and wring with extra enthusiasm, hoping to ask Shirley for a favor.

"Okay, Koko. What do you want?"

I hesitate. "Can I wear your cowboy boots today?"

"No."

My hopes sink.

"Why?" she adds, wringing socks.

"I just feel better when I wear them, like Dorothy did with her ruby slippers. You know, tap, tap, tap and I'm home. And . . . I want to wear them for the Girl Scout Songfest rehearsal this morning. We're performing it tomorrow."

She shakes her head. "Sorry, I don't think Mama's well enough for a sing-along."

"Songfest. It's called a Songfest, and it's not until tomorrow."

She wrings the last sock and hands me a wet shirt for us to wring together. "Why is this sing-along so important?"

I sigh. It feels like I have two mothers sometimes, always asking *why*. "I can earn points toward a Music Appreciation badge."

She throws a shirt into the basket. "Why work so hard on those badges, Little Frog, just to be a train greeter since, you know . . ." She gives me a side glance. "Since Pop won't be on a train for you to greet."

I bite my lip and pretend I don't care. "Oh, I'm not bothering about that train greeter stuff anymore."

She stops wringing. "But what about the other fathers and mothers and children who'll need greeting, Koko? And soldiers, like George. What about him? He'll be back after boot camp before he's shipped out."

I hate to admit it, but my sister's right. I hadn't thought of how others would enjoy being greeted. I reconsider trying harder to be a train greeter, but then quickly dismiss it. "Mitzi's going to be chosen, anyway."

She huffs. "Who says? You have just as much of a chance as anyone, Koko."

This isn't my old sister or new sister. This is someone else who's making me realize how much I miss the idea of not only greeting people—especially Pop—

but stepping outside the fence without someone trying to shoot me.

With the last sock wrung, she has me help her lift the basket of clothes. "Okay, you can go to your sing-a-thing rehearsal after you help me carry this back."

"You mean you'll let me wear your boots?"

"No. No, and triple no. I'm saving them for something special."

"What?"

"None of your bees wax. Besides, they'll slip off your feet for you to lose."

"I won't lose them."

Shirley gives me a sideways glance. "Um, does kite contest day ring a bell?"

I hate it when she's right. "Fine."

Her voice softens. "At least you asked this time."

It's a slow return to the barracks with a heavy basket until Marty swings around the corner. "Hey, hey, wha'da'ya say, dolls?" He takes the basket from us and lifts it to his hip like it weighs nothing.

Shirley does an instant marshmallow melt and she becomes *cra-zee*. "Oh, Marty, that's so sweet of you." Her swooning makes me sick to my stomach.

He looks at me. "Holy mackerel, Koko, you look cute with that bandanna." My hand automatically fiddles with a corner of a paisley scarf I've tied around my neck. "Hey, Shirl, would you like to go to a dance tonight? It's kind of a send-off for the guys leaving for Camp Shelby in Mississippi."

"Shurre, Marty, I'd love to go."

She's laying *cra-zee* on thick. "I think I'm going to upchuck."

"Shut up, Koko," she hisses. Yep. My grouchy sister is back again.

Mrs. Takata is waiting for us on the porch. Her roundness that usually looks so welcoming, is more hunched in concern. "Verree sorree," she says. "You Mama seeck. Hospital. "Verree seeck."

Without another word, Shirley fast-steps past Marty, leaving him holding our basket of wet clothes. She yells over her shoulder. "You coming or not, Koko?" She's already blustered around the corner before I can even get my feet in gear.

I count my steps to keep my knees from buckling. How did Mama get so sick so fast? I study the ground past barracks and up the knoll toward the hospital, pushing out the very real thought that she'd been hiding how sick she was from us.

When I catch up, Shirley's inside the hospital, looking blotchy-faced from crying.

"They've just told me we can't see her. They think she might have tuberculosis."

I sit on a chair to catch my breath. Nurse Kirk told the Pioneers about how tuberculosis is caused by bacteria in the lungs and how contagious it is.

Shirley pushes hair stuck by tears off her cheek. "She's had it before, you know."

Back then, Mama had Grandma Catherine to take

care of her, and then Pop when Catherine passed away. But now, it's been up to Shirley and me, and we've let her down.

My sister leans a shoulder against the wall. "If only Pop were here."

If she said it any sadder, I think I'd die. I touch her on the sleeve, but she pulls away.

Mrs. Takata catches up to us at the nurse's station, the same one where the welfare lady asked me questions about Baby. She speaks gently in Japanese, pulling us into her round softness. I have no idea what she's saying, but the sound melts into me.

When the door with Isolation Ward written on it finally opens, it's Nurse Kirk who walks toward us. "Sorry to make you wait girls," she says, looking at Mrs. Takata's hold on us, "but I see you're both in good hands."

"When can we see our mother?" demands Shirley.

"As I've explained, your mother will need to be tested, and until we get the results, she'll have to remain in the Isolation Ward. It's the rules."

Shirley presses her lips so hard they're white. "I'm tired of rules."

"Come," says, Mrs. Takata, guiding her away. "Mama be better, yes?"

"It's terrible to have this happen on such a beautiful day," the nurse says. "I bet you had something special planned to do with her."

"Oh no," I blurt. "The Songfest rehearsal!"

Shirley scowls at me with puffy eyes. "That's what you're worried about? Meeting with your stupid little brownies?"

Guilt rushes over me for being so thoughtless. "No, I didn't mean it like that."

"Go on then, go to your friends," she snaps, waving a hand in my face. "I don't need you, anyway."

"Good!" I snap back. "Because I don't need you either. You're the grouchiest sister in the whole camp. And I'm never speaking to you again!"

I want to lasso back the words as soon as they leave my mouth.

"Good!" she says.

"Good!"

I stomp away toward the place in the corner of our noisy camp where a puppy waits with kisses—where a special person watches a chocolate river and speaks to the sky.

Man Writing, Estelle Ishigo

JU-KU
Chapter Nineteen

Rows of green sprouts in the Victory Garden look happy.

But there's no sprout of a smile on my face.

Fifty-six, fifty-seven, fifty-eight . . . I breathe in the big Wyoming space, hoping to breathe in enough to give my worry more room, but the midway's crowded with people.

Always crowded with people.

Yama-san stands outside his door with a worried face. "So sorree, Koko-san."

"What's wrong?"

"Berkeley's gone."

If the world could open up, I've just been swallowed. Awful things are happening faster than I can catch my breath for. "Someone's taken him?"

He shakes his head.

"He's lost?"

"Not exactly." He leads me behind his barracks, which is open to the prairie, the wide-open prairie. He shows me a loose board that Berkeley's sleep box usually covers. "He's squeezed out between the planks."

"He's run away?" My voice cracks. I raise my hand to block the sun, looking out upon acres and acres of sage and tufts of shaggy grass. "Berkeley could be anywhere out there."

"Look." Yama-san points to the barbwire where Berkeley's frayed green and red collar that I'd made hangs.

I rush to the fence. "He could be getting bitten by snakes or torn apart by wolves." The thought lodges in my throat. I panic and flatten to the ground to slip under the wire to follow.

"No," Yama-san pulls me back.

"But he's probably just stuck in a sage bush. I'll be quick. The guards won't even see."

"Guards I'm not afraid of." He points toward the prairie. The tails of wild dogs appear and disappear as they run away from us over uneven ground.

"Berkeley's playing with that pack of dogs?"

"Sorry, Koko-san, but Berkeley's no dog."

My heart pounds. My fingers shake. I search his face for any kind of wink or lift of a smile to tell me he's joking. "Of course he is, silly."

He takes off his cap and runs his hand over his bald head. "No, uh, Berkeley's a wolf pup. Blue eyes—big feet. I wanted to tell you."

His words don't match what my head knows. Berkeley's a puppy. A sweet, cute puppy who makes me laugh.

"If a local rancher had found him first, he'd be dead already. Ranchers in Wyoming don't like wolves."

I remembered the howling of the wolves so close to camp. I cup my hands and shout. "Berk-e-ley! Berk-e-ley! Over here, boy!" I call him again.

Louder.

Harder.

Yama-san places his hand on my shoulder. "His family has found him. Let him go."

"But we're his family!" I snap, slipping out from under his hand and toward the fence.

"Berkeley needs his freedom. Be happy for him."

"No!" My voice is crackly and hoarse. I slip between the wires, determined, but a barb catches my coat.

Yama-san tries to untangle me from the fence. "He's with his real family now." His voice and grip are equally firm. "*Shikata ga nai*, Koko-san. This can't be helped. Wouldn't your father like to return to his family?"

Shock of what Yama-san has said strikes like lightning. The happiest moment I could ever imagine is having my father set free—how I wish we all could be set free.

Yama-san holds me mid-pose, halfway through the fence. He's waiting for me to let go, to shift my weight into his arms, on the side of the fence where Mama lies in a hospital bed, where Shirley's waiting. I let myself fall into his arms, knowing he's right. Painfully right.

BANG.

We both jolt at the rifle shot. The guard in the far look-out tower aims where the wolves are running. "Run, Berkeley, run!" I scream.

BANG.

Prairie dust kicks up from the ground where the bullet hits—misses—

BANG.

The wolves run, run, run for their lives. We watch until they're specks on the prairie. "Berkeley's gone for good," I whisper.

Yama-san ties Berkeley's frayed collar around my wrist. "Today, wolf was smarter than man."

I want to smile, but don't. *Shikata ga nai.* Some things cannot be helped.

NI-JU
Chapter Twenty

I barrel between people in the midway. Berkeley knew the importance of his family, and I do, too. Shirley's waiting for me. My teeth chatter from the cold—or from my next thought—that with Mama in the hospital and Pop gone, Shirley and I are alone.

Orphans.

Miss Frayne! If she finds out we're without parents, she'll be knocking at our door, for sure. The hurt inside me pounds against my chest demanding to be let out. I'm worried about Mama; Shirley's angry with me, and there's a hole in my heart that Berkely once warmed.

I turn a corner and trip over a vegetable crate and fall, scuffing my elbow. I brush away dots of blood and stand to kick the crate, like it was *its* fault for being in my way.

"What's the problem, young lady?"

I don't have to turn around to know who's speaking. It's the MP. The one who's always watching me, waiting for me to break another rule, the one who hates me. New tears lodge in my throat and a current of stinging anger circles inside me ready to hate him back. It's all his fault.

Leaving Mama's flowers to die in Clarksburg—his fault!

Breathing horse poop at Pomona—his fault!

Losing my letter to Pop—his fault!

Mama in the hospital?

HIS FAULT.

My breath is fast and tight. My feet twitch to walk away and ignore him, but one word from this man, and Miss Frayne will come and collect us. "My sister's waiting for me," I stammer. "I have to go." I turn to face him, but I forget about holding back. There's no way he can't read the hurt that's got to be plastered on my face.

The wind suddenly gusts, billowing the MP's shirt, flapping his pant legs, making him seem more of a giant man than usual. And then, off comes his Army cap. It sails through the air to plop in the dirt between us. A reflex has me stoop to catch it, but so does his.

We're face to face.

But his blue eyes aren't cold like before. They remind me of Berkeley. I quickly stand.

"Don't be afraid; I only want to help." His voice is the same, but gentler. He rises again to his full scary self, placing his cap back on his head. "I want to give you something."

I don't believe it could be anything good, but then he lifts his finger in the air signaling me to wait. "Came across this while doing rounds." He reaches into his shirt pocket and holds a crumpled envelope out to me.

The wind dies, as if on purpose. I'm grateful for the quiet, needing to balance my wobbliness with what he's offered me.

"Thought you might want it back."

I smooth my hand over the dog-eared envelope, not believing what I'm seeing.

"Have a girl your age at home," he adds. "Haven't seen her for a while, though. She's been ill."

Blowing around for weeks over rock and dirt has worn the paper soft to look ages old. I turn it over and over in my hands. Its thickness tells me the letters we wrote a month ago—Shirley's lock of hair—are still safe inside. The ink is faded, and in some places, completely washed away. But my father's name, written in my mother's hand, is still clear to read.

Mr. David Hayashi

Camp Santa Fe

Santa Fe, New Mexico

I open my mouth to say thank you, but nothing comes out. "I, I don't understand." I wipe tears that won't stop falling.

"I figured if my little girl had written me a letter and it got lost, she'd probably like to have it returned if it were found." He squats to be eye level with me. "And to be honest, all this, meaning the camp," he says, circling his hand in the air, "this isn't right what's been done to you all." He sighs. "It was just my job at first, but now I see things differently. When I see you, I see my own little girl, and I want you to know that I'm sorry, that I'm your friend if you need me to be."

I stare at the envelope through tears, but not from sadness, but because a piece of my life has been returned.

People are all around us in the midway, but I can't hear their voices for the pounding of my heart.

NI-JU-ICHI
Chapter Twenty-One

The light is on at 24-20. Shirley's there. The thought quickens my pace. I can't wait to tell her how sorry I am for speaking mean to her and show her the letter. The envelope tucked inside my shirt warms my heart against the chilly air. To think, the return of a little letter can mean so much to someone who feels they've lost everything. I'm reminded of those little lost things tucked inside Pop's sock. Someone might need them back.

Inside, the stove burns hot. Shirley's ripping down everything on her wall and shoving it in the stove. She yanks down the big Uncle Sam Poster that Marty gave her.

"Is that legal?" I say, taking off my coat. "Burning Uncle Sam?"

She turns, surprised to see me. Her face looks blotchy, as if she'd been crying. "You mean this?" She rips it, crumples it into a wad, and shoves it into the stove. "No. It's not against the rules." Her eyes narrow. "Where've you been?"

Her mood has gotten worse since she yelled at me to go away. "I was setting a wolf free."

"No need to lie, Koko. Mama's not here, remember?"

"For your information, I don't lie anymore. It's against the Code for Citizenship."

She pokes the fire. "You sound like Marty with all his talk about codes, rules and duty." She slams the stove door.

I didn't like being compared to Marty. "George is joining the Army. How come you're not miffed with him?"

"Who says I'm not? He'll be leaving his poor mother all alone." She plants hands on her hips. "Why fight for a country that's disowned us, Koko? Like Mr. Takata disowned his own son. Anyone who joins the Army is bonkers."

I think of the MP who returned our envelope. "Some Army people aren't bad."

"Why do you always argue with me?"

"I'm not arguing."

She gets quiet, holding a *Sentinel* article she's peeled from her wall. "Clarence Uno was a decorated American war hero from WWI," she says, sniffing. "He died right here in Heart Mountain, the prison the Army kindly built for him and his family. That's what the

Army's done for him." She gently folds the article for safekeeping.

"You're not just talking about Mr. Uno dying," I say, "you're talking about Mama. You're afraid she'll—you know—" I go to her, wondering if telling her about the envelope will lift her spirits. "Everything's going to be all right, Shirley."

"No it's not, and you're just as bad joining Girl Scouts. Do you think a bunch of badges proves you're good, Koko, like joining the Army is good for Marty and George?"

She's angry, which means she's exploding—on me, again. But I understand. I was with her when we were forced from our home, next to her when they jabbed our arms with fat needles against typhoid, back-to-back with her in a horse stall, and shoulder to shoulder on a long, scary train ride. She's angry and being mean, but she's my sister. She takes my hesitation as agreeing.

"Then I guess you do, Traitor Frog." She crosses the room to my cot. "It's time to come clean and quit pretending you're a Goody-Goody Girl Scout." She reaches under my mattress.

"No Shirley!" She holds me back with one hand as I push and grab, but she's stronger than me. Pop's sock rattles when she yanks it from its hiding place.

"Did you think I didn't know about this? Did you think Mama didn't know?"

I grab at it. "Please, don't!"

She swings it behind her. "All your confessions of

skipping school and hopping fences aren't worth anything if you still hide things. Mama's worn out over you, waiting for you to grow up, and now she's in the hospital—and it's all your fault!"

She walks to the stove. "I don't think a Girl Scout should pretend to be good and a thief at the same time." The stove door squeaks open.

"Nooo! You don't understand."

The fire licks and smacks.

"Oh yes, I do."

And with a flip of her wrist, she throws the sock into the fire!

NI-JU-NI
Chapter Twenty-Two

I grab my coat, slamming the door on Shirley, the destroyer.

The wind smacks my face with cold. No more counting steps. No watching the ground. I walk to the end of our barracks, turn the corner and stop. I pull my hand from my pocket and the peachy origami heart pops out. I'd forgotten it was there.

I unfold it and my words to Pop spill out in front of me all wrinkled. It's not a heart anymore. Not a family. Not lucky. It's just a worn-out peach can label covered in spiderweb creases. I rip it, one strip after another, throwing its bits out for the wind to carry away. I lean against a barracks wall and slide to the ground. Just when things seem to be looking up, they crash to the ground. I tent my head over my knees.

I hear someone running and look up to see Shirley

rushing around the corner. Her worried face turns to relief when she sees me. "There you are."

I rest my head back on my knees. "Go away." I swear never to lift my head to look at her or speak to her ever again.

Her shoes pivot in the crusty ground, and she sits next to me, shoulder to shoulder. "I'm sorry, Koko."

I don't want to hear sorry.

"I shouldn't have taken it out on you."

"Ha!" I say into the echo chamber of my pants.

She heaves a big breath. "I was wrong in saying all those mean things.

I'm too tired to forgive.

"You know, Mama wouldn't want us angry with each other."

I lift my head. "Double ha! You've been angry with me since we got here, so why change now? Admit it. You hate me!" I push my head back into the bend of my arm to squeeze away the pain.

She shifts closer. "I was ashamed the moment I said those things to you."

The last bell for mess hall rings and I hate the sound of a normal day when nothing, nothing's normal.

"So much has been taken from us, Koko, and I always take it out on you. But when I heard Pop's sock crackle in the fire, I realized that *I'd* become the one doing the taking." She touches my arm. "Please. I'm so, so, sorry."

I knew she was . . . I could hear it in her voice. I lift my head to look into my sister's eyes. "So, what happened to make you so angry this time?"

"At the hospital after you left," she begins, "the nurse told me Mama could die. *Die*, Koko. Like she needed to say that word because she thought I didn't understand English or I wasn't capable of knowing just how seriously ill Mama was. Me. A person who knows exactly what it means to lose everything—and she, a *hakujin*, who hasn't lost a single thing—had the nerve to tell me my mother could *die*."

She hiccups out a sigh. "But the nurse was right, and I'm still scared since the last time she was sick that she could—you know—

All the bossy, mean things Shirley ever said to me melt away. The burden of responsibility weighs heavy on Shirley, who's had to sometimes take over as mother and father, and I haven't helped. I lift my head and let out a shaky breath. "It's okay. I understand."

Her eyes are glassy. "We have to stick together, Koko."

I pull my coat tighter to stop shivering. "It won't be easy. If Mama has TB, she'll be in the hospital a long time."

"Yes. I know."

"It means that the lady from social welfare services, will be coming around. And I happen to know that children without parents get . . . get fostered out."

Shirley looks ill. "Fostered out?"

I stand, brush myself off. "Yeah, we'd be orphans."

I offer her a hand up when I spot something swinging from her hand.

Pop's sock.

"Sorry," she says, lifting it between us. "It's singed a little."

A wave of tenderness, invisible and kind, soaks warm into my bones. I throw my arms around her. "Oh, Shirley! You're like the moon god that saved Moon Rabbit from the fire."

"What?"

"You know, the story about Moon Rabbit? Didn't Yuki tell you about it?"

"No. But I definitely don't want to hear about a poor rabbit getting hurt."

"Yeah, but that's the point, Shirley. It's not the end of the story for Moon Rabbit. He gets saved, and lives!" I look inside the sock. Everything's safe. "You don't know it, Shirley, but I have something important to do with this."

"It's *we*, Koko." She puts her hands on her hips, but she doesn't look very bossy with a runny nose. "*We* have something important to do." She brushes herself off, too. "Though, I can't imagine what kind of trouble you're getting me into."

久 久 久

Before bed, I show Shirley the crumpled envelope the MP found.

Her fingers smooth over Mama's writing as if it was magical. "She'll be so surprised that our letters, after all this time, have found its way back to us." She's quiet for a moment. "I wanted so much for Pop to have a lock of my hair. I don't know why."

I remember how important it was to send Pop my letter. "You just wanted him to know you hadn't given up hope, Shirley."

We place the envelope next to Pop's watch, giving it a winding. *Tick, tick, tick.*

"I'm hitting the sack," Shirley says. "Big day tomorrow, skipping school and all."

We want to have everything in Pop's sock returned before Miss Frayne knocks at our door. "I have homework to finish tonight, but I'll be right behind you."

She rolls over and closes her eyes. "Okay, but I need sleep. If I'm headed for trouble tomorrow, I want to look my best."

I pull a sheet of paper from my book bag. I won't have time tomorrow to finish it, and the flag ceremony is Tuesday. I write the only words I can think of for Miss Percy's *American I Admire* assignment.

Koko Catherine Hayashi
The Photographer of Clarksburg

The photographer of Clarksburg is an American I admire because he can freeze history with one click of a button. With his camera, brides and grooms stay happy forever, babies never grow up, and blooming flowers never die. He says a good picture makes you curious, and a great picture makes your heart swell like the Pledge of Allegiance. He says a picture needs a spark of life, so smile big.

My homework's done, but it still breaks Miss Percy's one rule about it not being about a member of my family. One last sheet of blank paper remains. I smooth it open. But even if I used it to write another letter to Pop, the most important thing to tell him is something I don't want the WRA to read:

Dear Pop,

Mama's in the hospital, and Shirley and I are alone. Hurry!

I wrap my blanket around me and look out the window. The cold snap has delivered gloomy faces to the people passing by. The evening curfew siren sounds off. Spotlights switch on. One by one, unit lights blink out. Not far off, a record plays for the soldiers' send-off dance.

Beyond the camp, the moon shines on the prairie's darkness. I imagine Berkeley howling to it. Even the man on the record sings to the moon, but to the singer, it's not a heavenly body floating in space, it's someone he loves. I search for the rabbit that must be there.

And, as if I'd been looking at it my whole life, the outline of a fluffy rabbit appears.

My finger circles my eye. I focus the shot. Wait for the spark. Snap. "Gotcha."

NI-JU-SAN
Chapter Twenty-Three

Wake-up noises bounce across the beams. Stove doors bang, mixed with coughs and yawns, and the feet of Mrs. Yasaki's toddlers *beat-beat-beating* on the floor.

Today's mission: return everything in Pop's sock before this afternoon. Miss Frayne makes her family rounds in the afternoon.

Shirley's cot is empty. Hot water is in the kettle for morning tea, and the room is toasty warm. On a chair by the stove, she's laid out fresh clothes for me Mama-style, a flat little me all clean and smooth. Mama's not here, but Shirley keeps her close by doing those things our mother finds important. In the lap of the other me lays a note.

Dear Koko,

I've gone to the hospital to check on Mama. Maybe they'll let me talk to her. Meet you here later to go to mess.

Love, Your Sis

Her words latch a hold on my heart. I sip tea, *aaah-hh*. Steam rises from my cup, but something Shirley said to me has left a little cloud over me. She thinks those things I have in Pop's sock are stolen.

The door opens. Shirley's hardly inside when I ask, "Did you see Mama?"

Her face tells me no. "Test results won't arrive until late this afternoon. I'll check again then."

I throw on my coat. "Then let's get going."

First stop: The canteen.

Issei are playing *gō*. When I hand them all their stones, they get excited and urge us to stay. Shirley says, "Why not?" Though the *Issei* try to use English for our sake, pretty soon they fall into the feisty *rat-a-tat-tat* of excited Japanese outsmarting one another's moves. They don't even notice when we slip away.

Second stop: My school.

I don't know which marbles belong to which boy. We scatter them under the window where they always play and hide around the corner until recess.

"Holy cow, guys!" I hear Kenny say. "I found my cat's eye marbles!"

One of his friends asks, "Wanna trade?"

I suddenly regret giving up the cat's eye. It looked like a whole other faraway world whenever I stared into it. But when I hear Kenny's answer I'm glad I didn't.

"No way. Marty gave these to me when I was little. From now on, I'm gonna take better care of them."

"Let's hope Kenny does better than his brother at keeping promises," Shirley whispers. "Marty spouts off rules, but he's not too good at remembering them."

We lean against the tarpaper to warm our spines. "What rule has Marty forgotten?"

Shirley sighs. "The honesty rule. Remember Yuki telling us her parents were strict? Well, yesterday, on the way back from the hospital with Mrs. Takata, I saw Yuki and Marty together behind one of the barracks. Um, very together, if you get my meaning."

"You mean, k-i-s-s-i-n-g?"

"Yep. The grown-up kind."

"Marty's a fathead, Shirley."

She chuckles. "But you were right about him. He only invited me places so Yuki could tell her parents they were babysitting instead of . . ."

"K-i-s-s-i-n-g!" We both chime and laugh.

The bells for lunch ring. "C'mon," she says, "I'm hungry."

Shirley drops her sandwich after one bite. "I hate baloney. It reminds me of the train ride here."

I jab at my beans. The room is filled with the drone of people talking. Shirley's staring into her plate. "What are you thinking?" I ask.

She shifts in her seat. "Look, Koko. It's great what we're doing, but I've got a math test this afternoon. It might raise suspicions if I'm not there, right?"

Her warning sits heavy in my stomach like the

sandwich I ate too fast. I weigh her words against our important mission. "And I have my Girl Scout Investiture tonight."

"Investiture? Tonight?"

"Yeah. It's something all Goody-Goody Girl Scouts go through."

"Sorry for calling you that."

I lift a shoulder. "Be sorrier for calling me a traitor frog. I hate traitor frogs."

Shirley chuckles, and it's good to hear her laugh. "Okay. Your turn, Koko. What are you thinking?"

I'm not sure where to begin. Slowly, I pull out what's left in the sock and tell Shirley how I found each item, including the stories of the things we've already returned, about Berkeley, and Mickey's cap. By the time I finish, the mess hall is nearly empty.

"So, you weren't lying," she says. "You really took care of a wolf cub?" She laughs. "You certainly deserve a badge for that."

Wolf Badge: Check.

"It was wrong to call you a thief," she adds. "It's not a crime to care." She stands, handing me plates to carry. "I meant what I said. We're sticking together, Koko. After school tomorrow, I'll go with you to ask Mr. Oyama what block the little girl lives on so we can return her ribbon. And since the lighter is something Mama wouldn't want us to have, I think it would be better to drop it off at the Lost and Found, okay?"

We turn in our dirty plates and head out. "But the comb and Micky's cap are up to you to return." She gives my shoulder a squeeze goodbye.

"Good luck on your test," I add, wishing luck will be with both of us. I know it is and touch the lost letter I'd placed in my pocket.

If a letter can change into a heart, and a rabbit can live on the moon, then I can believe my family will be together again soon.

久 久 久

I check the sky like everyone's been doing lately. Snowstorms invade unannounced like toothaches. The sky is bruised with storm clouds. It's a sign—a good sign—that Miss Frayne won't be counting heads in the rain today.

First stop: To return the comb. I'm guessing it belongs to Marty and Kenny's mother, Mrs. Okamoto. At Christmas time, I remember her struggling with the wind to keep the recreation door open for her husband, Santa Claus, to deliver his big bag of presents—mittens, skates and candy. I'd found it sticking up in a mound of snow just outside the door.

Her eyebrows knit together when she answers my knock. "Why aren't you in school?" I can see she's busy hanging laundry inside her unit, and still more in her basket yet to go. I'd better be quick.

I hold out the comb.

She stares. Blinks. "Where did you find . . ." She takes the comb from my hand. "Oh my goodness.

This was a gift to me from my friend before I left for camp." She rubs her thumb over the pearls, like I did just a moment ago when I told it goodbye.

"Losing it felt like I'd lost my friend." She closes her eyes. "Thank you, Koko. Thank you very much for finding it."

She offers me tea. "Oh, no thank you, Mrs. Okomoto. I have to go." I tighten my coat around me on my walk back to 24-20, wanting to hold in the tingle of good feelings.

I have one more thing to do before Shirley returns from school. My steps slow. It was easier returning Mrs. Okamoto's hair comb, but Mrs. Takata is a close neighbor. What will she think when she discovers that all this time, I've held something important from her?

I make a fire in our stove like I've seen Shirley do a hundred times. As the flame grows, an idea grows too. I roll up my Arts and Crafts project, and after a big breath, I step across the hall to knock on Mrs. Takata's door.

"Koko-san," she says, looking concerned. "You okay, yes?"

"*Hai*," I answer. I hold up the pillow-sized quilt, needle, and some yarn to mime that I need help.

"Ahh, yes, yes," she says, and waves me inside. She pulls two chairs together and shows me a special embroidery stitch that looks like plants bending in the wind. They'll be plants for the Victory Garden that's in the window view of the quilt. I couldn't have a scene of Heart Mountain without its garden.

An hour later, my stitches look funny. I'm nervous about what to say to Mrs. Takata. I pull them out and start over. Twice I prick my finger and notice that blood has been smeared under one of the embroidered leaves. I look at a clock. Shirley will back any time.

A few minutes later, we're finished. Mrs. Takata holds up the quilt to show what we've accomplished. In an instant, I know I'll give it to George, like the white sashes the tiger women in camp gave to the soldiers, except these stiches will be from me.

"*Arigato gozaimásu.*" As I bow to Mrs. Takata, the bulk tucked under my waistband pinches me. I'd almost completely forgotten why I came. I pull out Mickey's baseball cap to show her.

Her smile drops.

I bow again, holding Mickey's cap out on open palms. "*Gomen nasai,*" I say, slowly, hoping Mrs. Takata will somehow understand. I am sorry. I feel the cap lift from my hands.

"*Hai.*" Her smile is as bright as a thousand candles glowing on a birthday cake.

She brings the cap to her nose and closes her eyes, like she was breathing in all of Mickey's dreams and wishes. "Verree good."

A knock at the barracks door spoils the moment. When I hop to open it for Mrs. Takata, all the weight of living here being lifted for just a moment, is suddenly sucked out the door.

Miss Frayne has come knocking.

VOL. II No.14   2 Cents Within City 5 Cents Elsewhere

Eight Couples Seek To Adopt Baby

Eight big-hearted couples are vying for Heart Mountain's Lincoln-day baby, announced last week as up for adoption. Virgil Payne of the social welfare department indicated that the successful couple will be named soon.

NI-JU-YON
Chapter Twenty-Four

Mrs. Takata waves for Miss Frayne to enter, smiling and bowing. It's too late to warn her about the social worker, and too late for me to slip away. The woman with trouble on a clipboard is here. I step aside.

"Brrr, blizzard's coming," she says. "And it's May, can you believe it?" She looks at me, and then glances down at her clipboard. "Hello, Koko. Number 20395-D, the youngest of the Hayashi family?"

I nod.

"I'm here to speak with you."

My breath quiets to the point I don't think I'm alive. Mama must have TB and Pop must not have proved his innocence. Shirley and I are orphans.

"But first," she adds, "I must speak with Mrs. Takata." She looks at my neighbor. "Number 44823, the Takata family?"

"*Hai,*" she answers. "*Takata.*" She invites Miss Frayne in, miming to her if she wants tea.

Miss Frayne waves her hand. "Oh no, no thank you. I'm here on business. Miss Makabe is going to help me this afternoon with translations, but I was in the neighborhood and with a storm on its way, I thought I'd stop by while I was here and talk with you about an important matter that really can't wait."

I don't know how much English Mrs. Takata understands, but Miss Frayne is talking as if she thinks she understands a whole lot. She looks at her clipboard. "So, your husband applied for repatriation to Japan, correct? And he took your youngest son, Mickey, with him?"

Mrs. Takata is silent, looking confused. She doesn't know the trouble she's in.

Miss Frayne says, "Do-you-un-der-stand-me?" as if Mrs. Takata was deaf.

"Can't you see you're scaring her?" I'm surprised my thoughts came out as real words. "She doesn't speak English, you know."

Miss Frayne must have people pipe up at her often. She doesn't get angry. She sighs and turns to me. "Can you translate for me, please?"

I'm stunned. The most truthful answer would be *no*. Mitzi would say *no*. Shirley would say *no*. Mama, *no*, but something tells me I can help.

"Of course I can translate," I say, as easy as pie.

Miss Frayne is relieved. "Oh, thank you, if you don't mind, that is." She again turns to Mrs. Takata.

"Now, in addition to your husband and son leaving, I understand that your eldest son, George, has joined the Army?"

After a moment, Mrs. Frayne looks at me, waiting.

My insides are shaking.

"Aren't you going to translate my question?"

I step toward Mrs. Takata, hoping I'm wearing a *kabuki* face that tells her, *I don't know what I'm doing!*

"*Obaaachaaan.*" Honorable grandmother stretched out sounds like a good start. I look at Miss Frayne who's still waiting.

"*Watakushi ni tegami ga kiteimasu ka?*" I've stood in Mr. Oyama's post office line enough times for me to have learned, "Is there any mail for me?" I repeat it slow so it sounds like as much translated words as what Miss Frayne used. Whata-kooshee-nee-teh-gah-mee-gah-keetae-mah-su, kah?

Mrs. Takata looks down. She must be thinking I'm crazy. "Ah, *hai*," she answers, following with flowing Japanese that I don't understand but sure sounds good. She lifts the picture frame of her sons and cleans the glass with the edge of her apron. In any language, we know she's a mother whose family has been torn apart.

"Does she understand?" asks Miss Frayne.

"Yes, Miss Frayne." I squeeze Mrs. Takata's hand, rough from years of farming in the America that promised a better life if she worked really hard.

Miss Frayne turns to me. "I know this is difficult

for her, Koko, but it's important that you translate this next part exactly right." She clears her throat and continues. "I'm sorry, Mrs. Takata, but there's a family of four arriving from the Minidoka Camp. They have a little boy who's ill, and we have a better hospital here at Heart Mountain for his treatment, so . . ."

Her voice trails off softly, sounding like a person who cares. She's not who I imagined her to be.

Mrs. Takata waits.

Miss Frayne waits.

It's time for me to translate, but I have no idea what to say. Underneath the quiet in the room, there's a pushing and pulling, like the ebb and flow of water, like Yama-san's spring sea *haiku* that I've recited a hundred times. Then, I get an idea.

"haru no umi" I say.

hinemosu notari

notari kana"

I repeat the poem, changing inflection here and there so it sounds like enough words are spoken to match Miss Frayne's. Mrs. Takata dabs her eyes. "*Hai,* Koko-san." We both sense each other's sadness in knowing what question Miss Frayne is building up to: Mrs. Takata will have to move.

My ploy suddenly feels like a mean thing to do. I can't translate. I'm stuck in something I thought would help Mrs. Takata, but now I don't know how to make it all end right.

Unexpectedly, Miss Frayne clasps Mrs. Takata's

hands. Her once piercing eyes have softened, her once stern face is curved into understanding. "I'm sorry," she says. "You have to move, but I'll do everything I can to help in the transition."

In that moment, the wind smacks against the barracks, rattles the window, and howls as if it agrees with me on how wrong this is: None of us should have been forced to move in the first place and then forced to move again and again. We've moved enough.

It snaps me into action. Words tumble out. "But Miss Frayne, didn't you hear?"

"Hear what?"

"Well, it's been settled already." A wave of warmth springs from my feet and spirals up to wrap around me like a warm blanket.

"Settled? What's settled, Koko?"

I don't know how upset Shirley will be when she finds out what I've done, but I have to do it. Now. "That Mrs. Takata is going to live with us."

Like on cue, Shirley and George burst through the door, along with a cold gust of wind. Their laughter dies when they see us.

"Hey sis," I say before either of them speaks, "I was just telling Miss Frayne here, the camp's *social worker*, about the good news."

"Good news?" Shirley's face goes blank.

George's, too.

"You know, about George's mother?" She's bound to think, at first, that it's the old me leading her into trouble. I hope she knows by now that I've found a new me, one with rules that I'll never have to hang my head in shame for following. I smile in a way for her to get the hint to play along. "You remember, don't you? That she'll be living with us after George leaves for the Army?"

Mrs. Takata steps close to George, speaking excitedly in Japanese. He listens carefully, his eyes widen, his mouth opens in an "O", and his head starts nodding like a bobbing-head toy. "Oh, yes, Miss Frayne, it's absolutely true. We gave the paperwork to your office just this morning." Still nodding, he looks at Shirley. "Right, Shirley?"

She catches on, and nods as she steps over to Mrs. Takata. "Yes, absolutely. We want Mrs. Takata to live in our unit with us."

Mrs. Takata is nodding now, too, and smiling. I don't know how Miss Frayne can suspect anything wrong with all the nodding in the room. And then Shirley throws me a glance. "In fact, my mother and I were just *discussing* it this afternoon."

My skin tingles. Shirley's talked to Mama, which means—No TB!

"And she's sure our father, when he gets here, will agree it's a wonderful idea."

Miss Frayne stands, pleased. "Well, this is good news, and good news is something I don't often get." She turns to me. "Thank you for translating, Koko."

Shirley's voice hitches up a notch. "Translating?" But—

"Otherwise," Miss Frayne continues, "I don't know what I would've done." She smiles in relief and then glances at her clipboard. "Now, that brings me to the second reason I've come knocking at your door."

I blink, confused. With Mama getting well and adding Mrs. Takata to our family, the conversation I dreaded having with Miss Frayne shouldn't be happening.

"I wanted you to be the first to know, Koko."

I look up. She's smiling and doesn't seem nearly as tall as before.

"Eight couples applied to adopt that little baby girl you found. I just wanted you to know that we have a perfect family to adopt her!"

I'm relieved and happy all at once. I don't have to worry about visits from Miss Frayne, we won't be moving, Mama's getting better, and Baby will have a home.

Everyone's talking all at once with excitement, and it doesn't matter to any of us, that in the middle of May, the frosty winter wind is having one last word with spring.

NI-JU-GO
Chapter Twenty-Five

Maybe Emily Dickinson knew about Wyoming, after all.

And still the pensive spring returns,
And still the punctual snow!

Freezing wind rattles our floors. Winter has tricked us.

A Wyoming blizzard gave no warning, like the one that hit in September after we first arrived. It had gotten so cold that some said the cows of local ranchers froze standing up. The little sprouts in the Victory Garden will be dead by morning.

Shikata ga nai. It can't be helped.

Miss Makabe's sticking to her schedule, though. She dropped off a khaki skirt and shirt for me to wear tonight. "Blizzard or no blizzard," she said. "You girls are going to officially become Girl Scouts tonight."

"I wish I'd thought ahead about having to wear a skirt when I decided to become one."

"Skirts are part of being a girl, Koko."

"But I like my overalls. Especially when it's cold."

"Think of it as a trade-off for being best friends with Mitzi. Remember, you did that pinkie-thing with her."

"It's the Double-Shake-Pinkie Promise."

"Yes, and you wouldn't want me to report to Mama that you broke a promise, right?"

We're smiling at the mention of Mama. Nurse Kirk said we'd be surprised by her improvement.

Shirley tilts her head to study me. "Hm. We'll have to do something with your hair, too." She wets a comb. "How about a fancy French braid?"

"Really? You'd do that for me?" Having my older sister do my hair will make me feel prettier. "But, let me finish my homework, okay?" *The Photographer of Clarksburg* isn't what I'll be turning in, after all.

Shirley waits, but drums her fingers on the table impatiently.

"Quit glaring, I'm almost done."

"It's just that George and Mrs. Takata are walking with us over to the USO building later, and we need to give ourselves plenty of time to get there in this blizzard."

"Okay, okay." I wiggle my pencil between my fingers and check what I've written.

Koko Catherine Hayashi
Tuesday, May 11, 1943
Americans to Admire

 Libraries have books with famous Americans to admire. But the Americans I'll never forget are the ones in and near my home at 24-20-D. They're the kind of Americans who can warm up a room in the coldest blizzard and make you feel like your family's just grown bigger than you could ever dream. They include my sister, friends, neighbors, and even people I thought hated me.

These are the Americans I admire most.

Finally. My assignment's done for the flag ceremony tomorrow, and it follows all the rules. Shirley goes to work as soon as I put down my pencil. "I wonder if Marty's lips will freeze to his bugle when he plays tomorrow morning."

"Yeah," says Shirley, picking up a section of hair. "It'd be a real shame if he used up all his pucker-power on Yuki." She steps back. "There. You look swell."

I run my hand over the smoothness of the braid. "Thanks, Shirley."

She stands with something hidden behind her. She brings her hands forward. Polished like new, are her cowboy boots. "I know it's not May 16th yet, Koko, but Happy Early Birthday."

My heart swells. I've never felt closer to my sister than right now.

"That's why I lugged them with me in the first place," she adds. "With our move to Pomona, and all the confusion . . . your birthday kind of got forgotten. They're yours, sis."

I think of how Shirley is like the moon god, testing me, saving Pop's sock from the fire, and now rewarding me with the best present she could possibly give. I hug her as hard as I can.

久 久 久

Mrs. Takata and George fall into step with us in the midway. I slip my hand into my pocket to touch the origami crane Mr. Oyama had folded for me. It's my new plan to get Pop home: fold a thousand cranes for a wish.

As I listen to our steps crunching in the snow, I think how far away from home our feet are and the many troubles that have fallen on us. But our feet, right now, are headed to a warm building where family and friends and neighbors are waiting. Tiny snowflakes tingle on my face like crystal thoughts. I think up my very own haiku:

troubles fall like snow

floating through angry wind to

melt upon my tongue

Everyone inside the soldiers' USO building laughs and visits like it's a summer picnic. Shirley sits at the back of the room. My new favorite MP stands by the door, cross-armed in his official pose. He spares me a quick glance and nod as I walk in. If he can still read through me, my insides are screaming *nervous!*

"Hey, Koko." Mitzi hurries to greet me, brimming with excitement. "I wasn't sure you were going to make it with your mother being sick and all."

"She'll be out of the hospital soon. But tell me about the Victory Garden. Is it dead yet?"

"*Tsk.*" She wags her head. "Oh, Koko. I keep telling you, the earth's not dead, and especially not our garden." She perks up. "Thanks to you."

"Me?"

"You were the one who collected all those cans for Mr. Yamamoto, right?"

I nod.

"He's shown my father all the sprouts he's been growing. There's enough to replant the garden."

I remember the boiler room Yama-san showed me. "But Mitzi, there won't be enough."

"Betcha a million bucks you're wrong."

It's my turn to look puzzled.

"You see, Yama-san didn't just have one boiler room of plants. He and his friends have *thousands* of sprouts tucked away in boiler rooms and hotbeds all over the whole camp! There are plenty of plants to save the garden!"

A May blizzard hasn't taken away our hope, after all. "It's a bet I'm happy to lose, Mitz." Looking at the brighter side of things even when all you can see is the bad, is what hope's all about.

She holds up her pinkies. "Friends don't owe each

other," she says, and we do our Double-Shake-Pinkie Promise.

Miss Makabe hurries to the stage, giving the Pioneers last minute instructions. Mitzi sits on one side of me. Ruth is on the other. I don't have time to get more jittery with nerves before the curtain opens.

The room is filled with friends and family. George is with his mother sitting in front of Shirley. Marty and Yuki sit with Kenny and his friends. Miss Percy's there with Miss Johansson, and Mr. Oyama waves. Yama-san tips his chin to me while trying to keep a new, wiggly puppy he's found under his coat.

I focus on the beautiful scene before me. *Snap!*

Cold air sweeps into the room. Mr. Henderson arrives with Miss Frayne close on his suit tails. "Good evening, everyone," he says, shaking hands as he makes his way to the stage. He checks the microphone, *thump, thump, thump,* and then grabs the lapels of his suit jacket before he starts to speak, elbows out, like they're suspenders. "Well, it's very nice to see you all together here this chilly evening. It's an honor for us to congratulate the soldiers of the Special 442nd Army Unit who'll be leaving soon to fight for their country."

Applause.

He talks about camp life, and all his usual gobbledygook, ending with his favorite line, "We are a smooth-running, orderly and progressive city."

Applause.

"And now, we'd like to honor these young girls

who have shown their love of country by becoming Girl Scouts." He calls Mrs. Somekawa up to the front. Miss Makabe sits behind us, holding our new silky flag from Ruth's mother.

"The Girl Scouts and Boy Scouts of Heart Mountain," he continues, "help keep the American spirit alive during these difficult times."

He pauses to nod at Miss Frayne at his side, and to my favorite MP. He clears his throat. "And information has been brought to my attention about a certain young girl who, through special effort, made a difference in her community. In fact, she's one of several Girl Scouts at Heart Mountain to earn the official title of Train Greeter."

Applause.

I know he's talking about Mitzi, and my face must be beaming with pride. She's the best Girl Scout in the whole camp, like I knew she'd be.

"She's delivered shoes to those housebound," Mr. Henderson continues, "found a complete set of Encyclopedia Britannica to donate to our library, and most importantly, rescued a little baby." His words finally catch up to my brain when he extends his arm in my direction.

He can't be looking at me.

"Koko Hayashi, would you be a good girl, and join me center stage, please."

He *is* looking at me.

I blink.

He waits.

But I don't always follow rules. I have my *own* rules to follow. I clasp Mitzi's hand on one side of me, Ruth's on the other. It starts a chain reaction and, pretty soon, all The Pioneers are holding hands and walking center stage to face Mr. Henderson, the boss of all bosses.

He twitches a smile. Mrs. Somekawa hands him my sash with all its badges sewn on and he lifts it over my head. His cologne smells spicy and clean, his hands gentler than I expect.

As it rests across my chest, it feels good, but not as good as Mrs. Okamoto's hair comb must feel to her, or Mickey's baseball cap to Mrs. Takata. It's not like the white belts stitched with a thousand red knots for the *yes-yes*-boys who wear them into battle.

I picture the sash going home with me someday—whenever that may be—and folded inside a box that I'll never open, even when I'm old. It'll remind me of what it felt like to be no one at all, except an enemy. I'll never tell anyone about it, or about Heart Mountain. I'll never speak of living behind a barbwire fence like a prisoner who never committed a crime. The sash isn't proof you're a good citizen when it can be stripped from you in a blink of an eye. But I *know* I'm a good citizen because my heart tells me so.

Mr. Henderson offers his hand. "Congratulations, Miss Hayashi. Good work."

Applause explodes like a good hard Wyoming rain after a drought. He presents each of us with our sashes.

Candles are lit around the room. Mrs. Somekawa nods to have the lights turned off, and on cue, we place our hands over our hearts and raise three fingers in salute.

On my honor I will try:
To do my duty to God and my country,
To help other people at all times,
To obey the Girl Scout Laws.

The lights flicker on. Applause, applause, applause—the ceremony's over.

And I'm crying.

But not because of anything happening that anyone can see. Nurse Kirk is with Shirley, and wrapped in Army blankets sitting next to her, sits Mama. She sees me and waves.

I hop off the little stage and run. "Mama, you made it!" I say, hugging her. "Did you know about this Shirley?"

"Sorry," says Mama. "I swore her to secrecy, because this secret is for both of you." Shirley and I exchange puzzled glances. Mama slides out a telegram from under her blanket. Shirley jumps to grab one side of it. I hold the other.

BE ON THE NEXT TRAIN FOR HEART MOUNTAIN. STOP. CAN'T WAIT TO SEE YOU. STOP. LOVE, POP.

VOL. II No 20 2 Cents Within City 5 Cents Elsewhere

Shivering Handful Witness Dedication of New Flagpole

The snow-laden north wind swept over the little company standing before the tall new flagpole; the snow greyed their hair and clung in little wet patches to their coats as they stood shivering in the slush underfoot.

At the foot of the flagpole the Boy Scout drums and bugle corps played earnestly, bare-headed and in short sleeves, and the wind lifted the bugles' blare, the booming of the drums and the crashing of the cymbals, and flung the militant and stirring dissonance like thunder over the prairie.

Presently, at a sharp command, two scouts marched front and center, the most beautiful of flags between them. Their fingers were stiff with the cold, and for a moment they fumbled with the halyard. Then slowly, the flag climbed the pole.

The snow had stopped. There was a tiny patch of blue above where the sky tried to break through the overcast, and the bugles sang out the clear notes of "To the Colors." Suddenly the wind caught the flag and it fluttered out, whipping proudly from the halyard, the white and red and blue rippling against the patch of sky.

That was how Heart Mountain's new flagpole in the administration area was dedicated Tuesday this week. To the bare-headed handful that stood in the slush to salute their flag, it wasn't just the cold that brought the tears to their eyes.

NI-JU-ROKU
Chapter Twenty-Six

The engine hisses and sputters. One of the Train Greeters can't contain their excitement. "It's here. It's here."

The train squeaks.

Jerks.

Stops.

People shuffle off the train. I see a man that looks like Pop, but I hardly recognize him.

The brim of his felt hat has lost its starch. Gray speckles his once beautiful dark hair. His shirt is worn thin, but I'd recognize the sparkle in his eyes anywhere. I'm laughing and crying at the same time, and run to shorten the distance between us, hardly believing this day has finally come. I hug him with every muscle in my body.

"Almost didn't recognize you," Pop says. "Wasn't looking for an all-grown-up cowgirl Girl Scout."

I giggle, leaning back on the heels of my boots. "Pop, you're in Wy-om-ming now."

We leave the train and head up the hill where Mama and Shirley wait at the gate. Pop's smiling, but quiet, as if his thoughts are rolled up tight like socks in his suitcase. He should take all the time he needs to unpack his thoughts.

Having to prove you love your country is hard work.

"So, your mother let you join Girl Scouts finally?" he says, touching my sash with his fingertips. "How many badges have you got there?"

"Six, and a Girl Scout Pin."

"I'm very proud of you."

At the gate, Mama and Shirley smother him in hugs he can't escape from. The last missing piece of the puzzle has finally fallen into place. Pop has filled the dark void in our hearts that we'd been missing.

We're a family again.

I step back and frame everyone's happy faces into the shot, but I don't have to wait for the spark. *Snap.*

Got it.

And I'll keep the picture to warm my heart for the coldest of any day ahead. I tap my boot heels three times. "There's no place like home," I say to myself, knowing home is found anywhere my family may be.

VOL. IV No 29   2 Cents Within City 5 Cents Elsewhere

Heart Mountain to Close Nov. 15 Director Urges All Residents To Take Action

From now until the closing date is only 17 weeks. Until Nov. 15, WRA will render all assistance it can to help people relocate.

There will be no service of any kind to Heart Mountain residents after Nov. 15. Mess halls will be closed on or before then, lights and water will not be available, the hospital will be closed and there will be no coal.

Any person who has not made a relocation plan should do so now while we have time to give their problems proper attention. ...Anyone finding himself in the awkward predicament can blame only himself.

THE LAST DAY
November 10, 1945

The War is over. In August, two terrible atomic bombs were dropped on Nagasaki and Hiroshima in Japan.

The sky here is as blue as ice, and the air is frosty, turning the tip of my nose cold. For some reason, the wind hasn't followed me on our last climb up Heart Mountain. From here, we have a view of the whole camp. It's deserted now. All ten thousand of us, gone. We're the last. Mama and Shirley are busy packing for home.

Home.

Charlene says I'll love the new high school they built in Clarksburg.

Pop stoops next to me, his pocket watch *tick-tick-ticking*. "There's a good shot, Koko." He points toward the garden, quiet with "punctual snow," like in Miss Dickinson's poem.

"I see it." I lift my Montgomery Ward camera that the WRA finally allowed me to have, and focus. My lens passes over where the cabbage patch once was—broccoli, watermelon, and beans. Three thousand tons of vegetables have been harvested from our Victory Garden these past three years. I spot the pipeline the evacuees finished. Like a straw, it connected Yama-san's chocolate milk from the Shoshone River to the garden. No one believed it could be done, a garden at the foot of a stony mountain where nothing had ever grown before.

I feel a spark. *Snap.* "Got it, Pop." We head back down the long hill to the train platform. The WRA has given us twenty-five dollars and a one-way train ticket to anywhere we want to go. The money falls short of any good will, but so did Executive Order 9066.

Mitzi says she'll write me as soon as she gets back to San Francisco. George said he'll write, too. He and his mother have been welcomed to settle in Cincinnati, but I think his letters will be mostly meant for Shirley to read. The Army gave him a Purple Heart for getting wounded at Pisa in Tuscany.

I don't know what the future may bring.

But if a letter can change into a heart, a rabbit can live on the moon, and a girl like me can find *gaman*, then I can believe broken hearts can mend.

AUTHOR'S NOTES

From the *hakujin*, J.C.:

Like the illusive image on the moon, the story of *Finding Moon Rabbit* offers only an imprint of the size, width and breadth of sacrifices a whole generation made for their country. If you're reading this, thank you for your interest in a time in history that was nearly lost to silence. Thanks to you, it may never come close to being lost again.

In 1942, over 120,000 persons of Japanese descent were removed from their homes for reasons of 'national security'. Most of them were school-age children, like you, infants and young adults not yet of voting age. All thirteen members of the Kato/Maekawa family lived behind barbed wire during WWII. The youngest was twelve. For decades after being welcomed into the family, I found the discussion of their experiences in camp a tender and taboo subject.

But if silence is a natural response to something terrible that has happened to you, then speaking up about it must be a natural path to healing. In a way, the silence was orphaning my children from their heritage, and from them knowing the courage, resilience and fortitude of their grandparents, aunts and uncles. I desired to one day create a safe place for them to connect to their history, whether cruel or kind, and still respect the family's privacy.

Koko's story began taking shape at the library.

John Tateishi, author of *And Justice For All*, contained the first narratives from internees who'd lived in camp that I'd ever read. In time, other Japanese Americans came forward. Now, hundreds of recorded oral histories have been collected by Denshō.org, a non-profit organization dedicated to preserving this history. One recording led me to Heart Mountain as a possible location for Koko's story. Since it wasn't one of the three camps where any of our family members had been held, it felt like a safe setting where Koko would live.

Once I knew *where* the story would unfold, I needed to decide *when* it would take place. I dived into reading *The Heart Mountain Sentinel* newspaper collection, also found at Densho.org. I loved the mixture of many Japanese cultures living in one camp, the children's exuberance in participating in the spring kite contests, how active the Girl Scouts were, and the camp's determination to grow a giant Victory Garden in the dry Wyoming soil where nothing had grown before. Some of the *Sentinel* articles used in the story were edited in length, and may not appear sequentially, but are true in content.

Several times I shelved *Moon Rabbit*. It was hard to keep revisiting such a personal topic. But when its early draft received SCBWI's Karen and Philip Cushman's Late Bloomer's Award, it encouraged me to pull it out again and work harder toward telling the story better.

Eventually, our family also opened up, and I'm happily joined by one of its Yonsei (fourth generation) members, J.C.[2]. I may have shed a million tears, worn out the soles of my shoes in visiting all ten camps, and bought more research books on the internment than what I had space for, but the heart of *Moon Rabbit* didn't come into focus until J.C.[2] arrived with her pen and mouse. It seems appropriate that from the family's silent beginning, comes forward an advocate toward its healing.

Though Koko's story is fictionalized around reported events at Heart Mountain, there are some anecdotal family truths that inspired certain characters and scenes, but I'll let J.C.[2] tell you about those.

From the *hapa*, J.C.[2]:

There are many reasons why I wanted to be a part of this story, but one in particular is truly held closest to my heart: To help bring about healing to all the lives that were affected by WWII, to those Japanese Americans that were forced from their homes, and to the people who feel a connection with Koko and her struggle during very hard times.

I don't remember learning of the camps in school, and my father's family never spoke about what had happened to them. I think, for them, they didn't want to bring any negative attention to the Nikkei, both Japanese citizens and aliens alike. And it wasn't until I was in college that they opened up about their experiences. Once they did, I found my family's history rich with harrowing accounts of their stay in the internment camps, and some of this was channeled into Koko's story.

My grandfather was in fact disowned by his father for joining the Army, taking all of my grandfathers' siblings away to Tule Lake to be expatriated to Japan. Expatriated, as in revoking their American citizenship.

Like Koko, my grandmother's family was the only Japanese Americans living in a small northern California town. In a later interview, my grandmother, Mitzi Kato, mentions after arriving at the Merced Assembly Center, how remarkable it was to see so many together in one place and how hard it was adapting to group living in barracks with no walls or partitions.

Although I respect my family's decision to remain quiet about what happened to them during WWII, I believe the age of silence has passed. Events happening today echo the same hatred and fear towards Asians. Maybe it's time to reflect and ask ourselves, "How far have we really come?"

Right now, we can choose to come together, and amplify our collective voices. To lift our focus above hatred and violence. To let go of past judgements, our racial conditioning, and to stop the ghosts of our history from dictating our future. Let's use our stories to educate so that history doesn't repeat itself.

"It is necessary to work ourselves out of Narrative Scarcity: To combat racism by amplifying our stories of heritage and accomplishments, challenges and grit, inspiration, and culture." (Julia Huang, CEO,

Intertrend Communications, "Beyond hashtags: Solidarity against Anti-Asian violence", April 12, 2021, Campaign US.)

The Real People in *Finding Moon Rabbit*

Clarence Uno was a World War I Veteran and American hero. Back then, it was against the law for Asians to become American Citizens, but Congress had made him one anyway on June 24, 1935. He passed away in January 1943 while in camp. *The Heart Mountain Sentinel* stated that his death "was release from confinement, against which he showed no resentment, by a government he loved and served."

Arthur Ishigo and his wife, **Estelle.** Theirs was a love story. Biracial marriages wouldn't be legal in the U.S. until 1967, but Arthur and Estelle had been married in Mexico more than ten years before entering Heart Mountain together. Estelle was hired by the War Relocation Authority to sketch camp life. Some sketches from her book, *Lone Heart Mountain*, are included within these pages.

Baby. Perhaps the most important real person: She was born on President's Day, February 22, 1943 and adopted by a loving couple as recorded in the *Sentinel.* She reminds us to not forget the children left behind by war and disasters.

Acknowledgements from J.C. and J.C.[2]

Finding Moon Rabbit has taken on many shapes since its first appearance in the playground of children's writing. If not for the encouragement of author, writing coach, agent, and person extraordinaire, Joyce Sweeney, it would have never hopped forward. We're thankful to SCBWI for offering scholarships and awards to its members, such as the Karen and Philip Cushman Late Bloomer Award that *Moon Rabbit* received in 2015. Support for SCBWI members doesn't stop at the national level. Linda Bernfield, Dorian Cirrone, and Kerry O'Malley Cerra of SCBWI Florida and its team, then and now, all quietly rooted for *Moon Rabbit* when it regularly popped its head up at yearly conferences. Special thanks from J.C. goes to agent, Rubin Pfeffer, for championing and encouraging her writing, and to Rob Sanders, a critique group partner who always offered solid guidance, along with Madeleine Kuderick, Norma Fisher Liburd, Jane Jeffries and Sue LaNeve.

Burrowed for a time, recent violence against Asians brought *Moon Rabbit* back out into the light. Our part in helping to combat systemic racism is by amplifying stories of heritage and accomplishments. Years have passed since *Moon Rabbit's* first emergence and with it, new critique partners. Their fresh eyes brought new perspectives and new life to its pages. Thank you, Skywriters, Teddie Aggelese, Augusta Scattergood, Susan Banghart, Janet McLaughlin and Susan Lloyd-Davis. Your knowledge of storytelling and never-ending support has made a safe place for *Moon Rabbit* to once again emerge. Of course, none of these words of gratitude would be written here if not for brother, Bret Clark, and our publisher, Gary Broughman at CHB Media, who championed Koko's story from cover to cover.

Our immediate family circle helped nest *Moon Rabbit* into the palms of your hands. We'd like to shout out to Uncle Tak. If not for you, we would have never known details of the Kato family's arrival at Tule Lake. And to Auntie Sue, who was the youngest family member to go to camp: Thank you. Your feistiness and robust nature sparked Koko's determined and lovable character. Donna and Kelly made Moon Rabbit an intimate family affair with their touch of art and photography. And our very own Beyond Barbed Wire lecturer, Denny Kato, the "Asian dude cooking food" person of the family, helped keep camp facts straight while making sure his wife and kids always had enough homemade tsukemono (pickled cabbage) to top their rice.

Thirteen of our family members were forced into camps. Most of them were American citizens. We recognize the unimaginable sacrifice they made for their children and for passing on to all of us their legacy of fortitude, dignity, and emotional resiliency. It's our desire that *Finding Moon Rabbit* will not only inform our readers of this important time in American history, but for those who are enduring unbearable hardship today, to let you know you are not alone. May the stories you choose to share one day allow us all to see the world differently. Our support and *gaman* to all of you.

A CHRONOLOGY OF EVENTS

1843	John Manjiro, is the first Japanese national to live on mainland United States in New Haven, Mass.
1870	U.S. Congress grants naturalization rights to free whites and people of African descent. Japanese nationals were ineligible for citizenship.
1912	Juliette "Daisy" Gordon Low starts Girl Scouts and declares it a space for all girls.

1941

December 7	Japan attacks American military installations at Pearl Harbor in Hawaii.
	FBI makes arrests of suspected Japanese spies and traitors.

1942

February 19	**Day of Remembrance** Order 9066 is signed by President Roosevelt. It leads to the forced removal of 120,000 of Japanese ancestry from West Coast.
March 18	Order 9102 establishes The War Relocation Authority (WRA).

	Exclusion Orders are posted. Families must leave home for fifteen Assembly Centers.
August	Ten internment camps completed.
October	The first train of evacuated families from Pomona Assembly Center arrive at Heart Mountain.
	Population reaches over 10,000 at Heart Mountain.
November	Children report to school and Boy and Girl Scout troops are formed.
December	Construction of the barbwire fence around Heart Mountain begins. Three thousand people signed a petition against it as "an insult to any free human being, a barrier to a full understanding between the administration and the residents."
	Nisei boys age eighteen and nineteen must register for the Army.

1943

February	The Nisei are asked to complete the loyalty questionnaire which raises the "yes-yes" and "no-no" debates.

April	Plowing for Victory Garden begins.
May	Town councils of Powell and Cody pass resolutions against internees receiving special passes to enter city. It was quickly reversed.
1944	Five hundred Boy and Girl Scouts spend a one week hiking and camping excursion in Yellowstone Park.
1945	
April 12	President Roosevelt dies in office. Harry Truman becomes president.
May 7	German Army unconditionally surrenders to allies
August 6	Truman launches the first atomic bomb on Hiroshima.
August 9	**Second Day of Remembrance.** A second atomic bomb is launched on Nagasaki.
August 14	Japan unconditionally surrenders to allies, ending World War II.
November 10	The last train of Japanese families leave Heart Mountain.

1947	December 23 President Truman signs Presidential Proclamation 2762 granting a full pardon to the Nisei draft resisters.
1952	Congress passes Public Law 414 granting Japanese aliens the right to become naturalized U.S. citizens.
1969	Girl Scouts launches "Action 70," a nationwide effort to overcome prejudice and build better relationships among persons of all ages, religions, and races.
1988	President Ronald Reagan signs the Civil Liberties Act to compensate the people of Japanese descent who were incarcerated in internment camps during World War II.
	The legislation offered a formal apology, paying $20,000 in compensation to each surviving victim. The law won congressional approval after a decade-long campaign by the Japanese-American community.

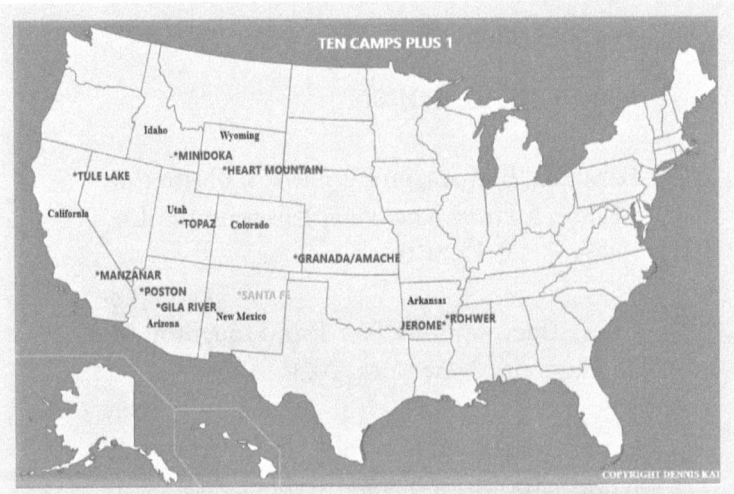
Map of U.S. government WWII Japanese internment camps

U.S. Dept. of Justice detention camp, Santa Fe, New Mexico

A Japanese American child, Heart Mountain internment camp.

FURTHER READING

Bazaldua, Barbara, and Willie Ito, Illustrator. *A Boy of Heart Mountain*, Yabitoon Books, Camarillo, CA, 2010.

Chee, Tracy. *We Are Not Free*, Houghton Mifflin Harcourt, New York, 2020.

Cushman, Karen. *War and Millie McGonigle*, Knopf Books for Young Readers, 2021.

Densho: *The Japanese American Legacy Project* is a digital archive of videotaped interviews, photographs, documents, and other materials relating to the Japanese American experience found at www.densho.org.

Mochizuki, Ken and Dom Lee, Illustrator. *Baseball Saved Us*, Lee & Low Books, 1993.

Nagai, Mariko. *Dust of Eden*, Albert Whitman & Company, 2014.

O'Connor, Barbara. *Halfway to Harmony*, Farrar Straus Giroux, New York, 2021.

Image Credits

12: "State of California, [Civilian Exclusion Order No. 78], City of San Francisco, California", May 15, 1942, by J.L. DeWitt, Lieutenant General, U.S. Army, Western Defense Command and Fourth Army, Courtesy of Online Archive of California, Japanese American Evacuation and Resettlement Records.

34: "A Code for Citizenship," 1943 Girl Scout Leadership Handbook (public domain).

124: Loyalty oath questionnaire, questions 27 and 28 for citizens of Japanese descent, 1942.

Estelle Ishigo Sketches: Ishigo, Estelle, *Lone Heart Mountain*, 1972, Book, Courtesy of the Library of Congress.

2, 212: Map of Heart Mountain. (pp.#77.)

68: Library at Heart Mountain. (pp.#46.)

87: Family in their unit. (pp.#26.)

95: Children with kite and poem. (pp.#1.)

107: Camp clean-up. (pp.#31.)

143: Man at writing desk. (pp.#49.)

Newspaper Articles: *Heart Mountain Sentinel*, Courtesy of the Library of Congress, Serial and Government Publications Division.

14: "10,000 Heart Mountain Residents Greet 1943 With Mingled Feelings," vol. II, no.1, January 1, 1943.

57: "Girl Scouts Take Orders for Cookies," vol. I, no.7, December 5, 1942.

96: "Victory Gardens to be Grown Here," vol II. no. 17, April 24, 1943.

170: "Eight Couples Seek to Adopt Baby," vol II. no. 14, April 3, 1943.

188: "Shivering Handful Witness Dedication of New Flagpole," vol. II no. 20, May 15, 1943.

192: "Heart Mountain to Close Nov. 15 Director Urges all Residents to Take Action," vol. IV no. 29, July 14, 1945.

J.C. Kato is recipient of the Karen and Philip Cushman Award for *Finding Moon Rabbit*, an active member of SCBWI, and Co-Editor of the Florida State Poets Association Anthology. Drawn to pay homage, she's visited all ten Internment Camps/Museums throughout the United States, including the DOJ Memorial in New Mexico, and twice to Heart Mountain. She lives in Florida with her family and Ewokie-looking dog, Poppet.

$J.C.^2$ is Yonsei Japanese American and though her pen name might leave most mathematicians scratching their heads, she thought it an equation just too cute to pass up. She's the proud daughter of hakujin, J.C., and lives in Florida with her rescue Pit Bull, who spends most of the day napping and scavenging for who-knows-what in the backyard. Aside from her full-time gig of counting beans, she spends her days devouring sci-fi books and practicing her newly found devotion to the study of Yoga, which works out when you're really twisted.

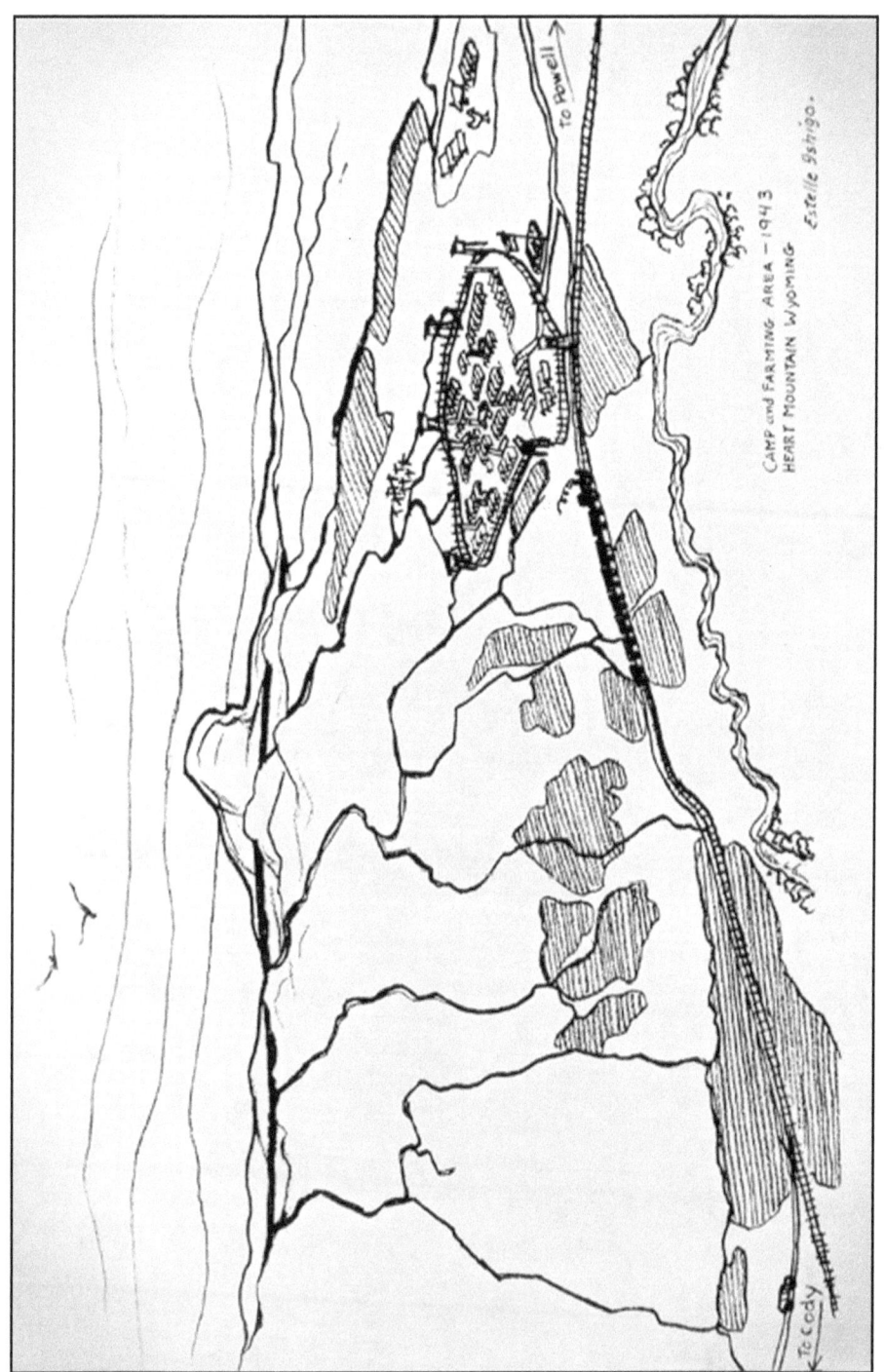

www.ingramcontent.com/pod-product-compliance
Lightning Source LLC
LaVergne TN
LVHW091546070526
838199LV00023B/550/J